The Island on Bird Street

 Uri Orlev

**translated from the Hebrew
by Hillel Halkin**

Houghton Mifflin Company Boston

Library of Congress Cataloging in Publication Data

Orlev, Uri, 1931–
    The island on Bird Street.

    Translation of: ha-I bi-Rehov ha-tsiporim.
    Summary: During World War II a Jewish boy is left on
his own for months in a ruined house in the Warsaw Ghetto,
where he must learn all the tricks of survival under
constantly life-threatening conditions.
    1. Holocaust, Jewish (1939–1945)—Juvenile Fiction.
[1. Holocaust, Jewish (1939–1945)—Fiction. 2. Jews—
Poland—Fiction. 3. World War, 1939–1945—Poland—Fiction. 4. Poland—History—Occupation, 1939–1945—Fic-
tion]   I. Title.
PZ7.0633Is   1984   [Fic]   83-26524
ISBN 0-395-33887-5
PA ISBN 0-395-61623-9

Printed in the United States of America
QUM 20 19 18 17 16 15 14 13

Contents

Introduction

Think of the city that you live in or the city that is nearest to where you live. Imagine all of your city occupied by a foreign army that has separated part of the inhabitants from the rest: let's say, everyone with black or yellow skin, or everyone with green eyes. And imagine that they are not only separated from everyone else but are imprisoned in one of the city's neighborhoods around which a wall has been built. Naturally, this wall would have to cut down or across certain streets and would sometimes even divide single houses and their yards in two. Inside the walled-off neighborhood everything remains the same: the movie houses, the schools, the nightclubs, the different stores, the hospitals. Yet because of the wall and the guards stationed at its few checkposts that can be crossed only by special permission, supplies have trouble reaching the stores and the peddlers who, young and old, increase in number day by day. And of course public transportation isn't what it used to be either. The private cars and the trolleys have disappeared and the streets are filled with "rickshaws" (sort of large tricycles that are pedaled by drivers sitting behind and have seats in front on which three skinny or two fat passengers can fit.)

If you were wealthy before the occupation you can still afford to buy what you want or even to visit the nightclubs. Although for that you have to be very rich and to watch out for the night curfew. And if you're brave or desperate enough you can try smuggling food from other parts of the city into your walled quarter. If you're caught, you'll be shot, even if you're only a small boy or girl. If you get away with it, though, you'll make a fortune overnight. Next time perhaps you can hire someone else to do the dirty work for you and not have to risk your own neck. You see, here, the difference between being rich and poor is not just a question of how you live or dress or eat. It is a question of life and death. The rich have food while the poor die of hunger and no one is able to help them.

I can remember my mother refusing to go out into the street because she couldn't stand the sight of all the children begging for bread when she had nothing to give them. Her first worry was for me and my brother, and every slice of bread she gave another child meant one less for us. And I remember how once on my way to "school," which was really only a little room with three students and one teacher, a man snatched a sandwich bag right out of my hands and swallowed the paper and the string together with the sandwich. It baffled me how he managed to get down the string — paper was one thing, but *string?* And then two well-dressed men came along and gave him a beating because he had stolen food from a well-dressed child.

Still, people married, quarreled, and loved. They even had children. And there were birthdays and toy shops and a bakery that belonged to an aunt of mine who gave me a pastry every day. There was a boy who lay for a long time on the sidewalk outside her shop until he died.

One day the occupation authorities decided to get rid of the inhabitants of the walled quarter. To send them far away. Today we know that they were sent to extermination camps. Eventually we who lived there knew too. But not at the very beginning. It was too hard for us to believe that civilized people like the Germans could do such a thing. It was hard to believe it even after witnesses escaped from the camps and told us. The city I lived in was Warsaw and the walled quarter was called the ghetto. That's where I was during World War II. But let's get back to our imaginary city.

Suddenly people begin to disappear from it. They take a small suitcase or a knapsack with them and the rest is left behind. Their homes remain as they were with their furniture, their clothing, their beds, and their books all in place. The front doors are left unlocked because that is the order that has been given. There's just no one living there. Not even cats or dogs, because there isn't anyone to feed them and they've left for other parts of town.

Another thing you won't find is radios. These were forbidden at the beginning of the occupation. And, of course, television hasn't been invented yet.

The occupying army wants to take whatever is left in the empty houses for itself, and so it leaves the wall standing and keeps the guards stationed at the checkposts. Inside the wall, the ghetto is like a ghost town. Only here and there a few little islands of life are left — factories in which people work for nothing in order to make things for the occupiers:

army socks, for instance, or boots, or rope, or brushes. And next to each factory is an apartment building for the workers.

My aunt, my little brother, and I lived in such a building for as long as the workers were allowed to keep children with them. By then my mother was no longer alive. I remember how my aunt used to send me, along with two men we knew, to search for coal in the empty houses that lined the abandoned streets. In those days we still heated our homes with coal in the winter and cooked on coal stoves in the kitchen. And, just like you'll read in this book, I went from building to building through passageways in walls and lofts and ran crouching when I had to cross a street. We were searching for coal, but wherever we went, I searched for children's rooms too, and when the men weren't watching, I entered them and looked for books and stamps for my collection. I couldn't take much because I had to return with a sack of coal on my back; still, each time I managed to come back with a new little treasure-trove that made my brother green with envy. I gave him all the duplicates, of course, and the books, though not before I'd read them first. *Robinson Crusoe* was one of the books I found this way.

Which brings us to our own book, *The Island on Bird Street*. The empty neighborhood you'll read about here is the ghetto. It doesn't have to be the Warsaw Ghetto, because there were other ghettos, too. But in this one also the houses have been emptied of food and people while everything else has stayed the same. Alex, the hero of my story, hides in a ruined house that was bombed out at the beginning of the war, although all the other houses around it are untouched and full of possessions. This house is really not very different from a desert island. And Alex has to wait in it until his father comes. But his father does not come back right away and Alex begins to wonder if he ever will. So he must survive by himself for many months, taking what he needs from other houses the way Robinson Crusoe took what he needed from the wrecks of other ships that were washed up on the beach. The difference is that Alex can't grow his own food, that he has to hide, and that he has no spring to get water from. But Alex can see the rest of the world through a peephole in his hideout, because the ruined house overlooks the wall that seals off the deserted ghetto. Through this hole he sees all the people who aren't shut up as he is, even if they too must live under a cruel occupation. He even sees children going to school every morning — and yet, although they seem so near, they are as far away from him as were the nearest inhabited lands from Robinson Crusoe's island. Alex has no man Friday either; he has only a little white mouse. And, yes, one more thing: Alex has hope. Because he is waiting for his father.

Uri Orlev
Jerusalem, 1983

The Island on Bird Street

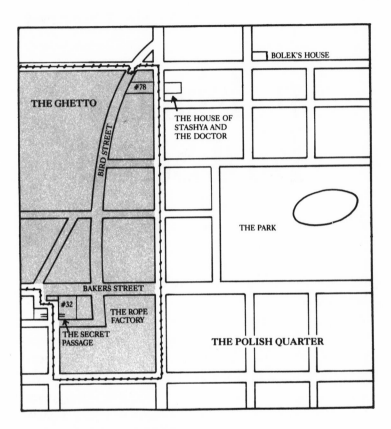

THE GHETTO WALLS

Father's Secret

I woke up. Father was sitting on the floor with a lit candle beside him. I was very sleepy and still in the middle of a dream. I yawned and tried to get back to it. Sometimes, if you're not fully awake yet, it works. Mother once told me that you can do it if you don't look out the window first. But there was nothing to see in the window now, anyway, because it was dark outside.

I wanted to know, though, what father was doing on the floor. He had some small pieces of metal. I could hear them clink. He wiped them and looked at them. And then he noticed me sitting up in bed. At first he covered everything with his hands, as though it were a secret. But then I knew what it was. I could see the trigger and the butt. Father had a pistol! Suddenly I was wide awake. Was he going to kill some Germans?

Mother still hadn't come back. She had gone to visit some friends in Ghetto A and never returned. That was a week ago, or maybe a week and a half. I didn't count the days, because it would have made me too sad. At first we figured that she had been caught and put to work somewhere near the ghetto. Then we thought that maybe she had been taken elsewhere for a few days. In the end we began to believe that she had been transported to Germany. Not many people ever got letters from there through the Red Cross, and even if they did, they never knew if the sender was telling the truth or had been forced to write what he or she wrote.

Father looked at me for a minute and then took his hands off the parts of the pistol. I started to ask him about it, but he put a finger to his lips — maybe because of the Gryns, who slept in the next room of the apartment that we shared with them. I got out of bed and went over to sit by the candle on the floor.

"Is it real?" I asked in a whisper.

"Yes," he said, smiling at me.

As though I hadn't known. Still, it was hard to believe. I had never heard of anyone in the ghetto having a pistol. And even if some people did, there couldn't have been many of them, maybe no more than two or three. Although the fact was that I simply had no way of knowing. Children weren't let in on such things.

"What are you doing with it?"

"Cleaning it and oiling it in case I have to use it."

"To kill Germans?"

"Yes, Alex," father said.

I winced. "Tomorrow?"

"No," he said. "Don't worry about it."

Father hadn't meant to tell me about the pistol, even though I helped him do everything. I helped him build the bunker with the Gryns, and the little hideout in the ceiling that we made just for us, in addition to helping just to fix things around the house. But now that I had seen it, he was ready to show me how to take it apart and put it back together, how to clean and oil it, and what to wipe the oil from before using it.

"How come you know all that?"

"I was a soldier once," he said.

"You never told me."

"It wasn't the happiest time of my life. I was lucky enough to make the army boxing team, but the other Jews had a hard time and I felt bad for them."

It was an Italian Beretta with seven bullets in its clip. Father took them out one by one and showed me how they were made.

He thought for a while. And then, as though suddenly making up his mind, he said, "I'm going to teach you how to shoot."

He did. And even today if someone were to wake me in the middle of the night and want to know, I could tell him without a single mistake: A 1934 Italian Beretta. Bore: 9 millimeters. Barrel length: 92 millimeters. Overall length: 149 millimeters. Weight: 680 grams.

After that first time, we sat on the floor night after night while I practiced assembling and disassembling the pistol. Father showed me one thing after another. How to cock it. How to open the safety catch. How to aim. He lay facing me with a piece of cardboard while I aimed at a little hole he had made in the middle of it. Then I pressed the trigger and said, "Bang!"

Father could tell by looking through the hole whether or not I was on target.

"Some day, Alex," he said, "these lessons may help save your life. Who knows when and how this war will end."

He sighed. The war was already three years old. It was

the Second World War. Father could remember the first. And once he kidded me: "With a little luck you may even get to see the third."

Was he wishing me a long life or just saying that this wouldn't be the last war? When I asked him he explained that when the First World War had ended everyone thought that it was the last, yet here we were in the middle of another. The difference was that then they didn't kill Jews. Not especially, that is, although Jews did fight in all the armies and sometimes even killed each other. My father's parents, my grandfather and grandmother, had even had some German officers living in their house who behaved very politely to everyone. It was strange to think about that. The worst thing they did was take all the bronze doorhandles and fixtures to melt down for their big guns. And one of them had wanted to be Aunt Lunya's boyfriend. That got grandmother mad. Why, though, had they been so nice then? Father didn't know. But maybe that was why no one in this war had wanted at first to believe that the Germans were really killing Jews and taking them away to special camps.

Father and I lived in a building a few attached houses away from a factory that made ropes for the German army. Early each morning father went to work in the factory and I went to the ceiling hideout, unless he decided to hide me in the bunker down below. It all depended on what rumors reached us that day. Sometimes he even smuggled me into the factory storeroom through hidden passages in walls and roofs. Old Boruch, the storeroom manager, taught me how to tie knots with different kinds of rope and talked to me about so many things that I was sure he must be at least as wise as King Solomon. I didn't tell him about the pistol, though, because father made me promise not to.

I hadn't known it until then, but father took the pistol with him everywhere. He had made himself a leather strap with a sling that fitted under his arm, and he kept the pistol in it. At night he slept with it beneath his pillow. He wasn't afraid that the Germans would find it on him. No German ever dreamed that a Jew working in a factory or walking down a street might be armed. Even when they rounded up Jews for transport by train to what they called work camps they never searched for hidden weapons.

Boruch watched the storeroom and made tea in a little electric kettle. He kept a list of the bales of rope that came in and went out. The bales were loaded by two workers from the factory onto a truck driven by a German soldier. Sometimes the driver was a blond soldier who used to offer Boruch cigarettes, although Boruch never offered him tea. Sometimes it was a redhead, who shouted at him and made him carry bales too. Now and then the redhead even kicked him. When they were gone, Boruch would wipe the sweat from his face, sit down with a groan, feel the inside of his left leg right above the shoe, and grumble something to himself.

One time I asked him, "Does your leg hurt you, Boruch?"

He looked at me hesitantly and rolled up his pants leg. Stuck into the shoe I saw a large kitchen knife. "Some day old Boruch is going to settle accounts with at least one German."

"Some day I — " I began to say and caught myself just

in time. I had almost given away the secret. "Some day I'd like a knife like that too," I said in the end.

"You're too small for such things now," he said. "But you'll get your chance when you grow up."

It wasn't that simple to kill a German. Not that it was difficult, because it would never have occurred to any German that a Jew might try to kill him. The German in charge of the storeroom, for instance, kept his pistol in a closed leather holster on his belt. He would have to open the snap before drawing it and by then Boruch could stab him. From behind would be easiest. It might not be the gentlemanly thing to do, but father once said to me that you didn't have to fight fair against the Germans because they were the first to break all the rules. Only father couldn't use his gun any more than Boruch could use his knife, because if anything ever happened to one single German in the factory or the street, the Germans would kill lots of men, women, and children to make sure it didn't happen again. A retaliatory action, it was called. And so no one dared do anything. How could you be responsible for so many lives just because you felt like killing a German?

"We don't even know for sure if the rumors of Jews being killed in the camps are true," father said.

"We do know," said Boruch. "I myself talked with a young fellow who escaped from such a camp. Didn't I tell you?"

Father sighed. He wanted to keep on believing that mother would come back.

"If you're so sure of it, Boruch," he said, "why don't you do something?"

"I already am," said Boruch. He winked at me. "I'm looking after your son."

Father went back to work.

One of the things I talked to Boruch about was Hitler. Boruch had never met him in person, but he had read lots of books about him. He had even read a book that Hitler wrote himself.

"Take Napoleon," he said. "Thousands of people were killed in his wars too. People died of hunger and disease. But Hitler is doing something that has never been done before. He is building factories in which to slaughter human beings like cattle. That is the difference." Each time he would end by saying: "That's why he'll lose the war and die like a dog. Germany will be razed to the ground and his name will be a curse until the end of time."

"It would be better," father said once, "if it were simply erased from all the history books. As though he had never existed."

"No, it wouldn't," said Boruch. "All this must be remembered so that other peoples will know what can happen when a madman is elected to be leader. And so they will realize that there are times when even children must be taught to bear arms."

I glanced at father.

If he and I had been with mother when she was caught, they never would have taken her anywhere. That's for sure. Even if afterward they had killed a whole street full of people.

2

Snow, and Are People Like Trees?

I had a little white mouse, the only one left of all the mice I kept as pets in our house. Not in our first house, of course. In our house in the ghetto, before the transports began.

Some people hate mice; some are afraid of them. But having a mouse for a pet isn't really very different from having a cat or a dog or a canary. It's just that mice are smaller, eat less, and are less bother if you know how to take care of them. Boruch, for instance, once confessed to me that he hated them. He didn't say it right off. At first he just told me not to bring my mouse with me to the storeroom. He said it would run away and that I'd never find it among all the bales of rope. So I told him that it came to me when I whistled and that I'd even show him. That really scared him, although, strangely enough, he wasn't afraid of Germans at all.

"No, thank you," he said.

He told me that there were gray mice in the storeroom that would kill my mouse. I had never seen any gray mice there, but he claimed that they lived in holes in the floor.

"But why will they kill him?"

"Because he's white."

"Maybe they'll make friends with him."

"Then you'll never see him again. He'll take up with some she-mouse and never come back."

"Maybe he's a she himself."

"Then he'll take up with some he."

So I left him at home. His name was Snow. In the morning I'd tell him that I'd be back late with father and that he shouldn't worry. It made father laugh to see me talking to a mouse. But I said, "You always talked to Rex." Rex was our dog. He died of old age after we brought him to the ghetto with us.

Father let me do what I wanted with the mouse.

He wasn't just an ordinary mouse either. He was a very smart one. That's why he stayed alive when all the other mice in the cage got sick and died. Father said that being immune had nothing to do with being smart. But the fact was that he was always a little different from the others. I had noticed it even before he was the last mouse left in the cage.

I don't know how I would have gotten through whole days without him, from early morning until dark, alone by myself in our ceiling hideout or down below in the bunker. How long could I just sit there and read? And father didn't always manage to find new books to bring me. Of course, if a book is really good you can read it a second and even a third time. Like *Robinson Crusoe*. Or *King Mathias*. But you can't just read all day long, every day. So when I couldn't read, I'd play with Snow. Sometimes I'd hide his food somewhere and let him look for it. I taught him that the game started when I whistled. He would begin to run around, sniffing everywhere, until he found the food. And he almost always did. Even if I didn't hide it all at once, he'd keep it up until he'd found it all, poking under all the rags and pillows.

When I talked to Snow, I knew I wasn't exactly communicating with him. I mean I knew he couldn't understand, even if he did listen. But it was better than having to talk to myself all the time as though I were crazy. I'd tell him that the war would be over soon and that then I'd buy him a nice big cage. And that I'd bring him lots of friends, males and females, because I didn't know which he was himself. You can't tell with mice. Even father couldn't tell.

I wasn't allowed out of the hideout until father came home at night and signaled to me. Even if he didn't come home all night long and all the next day, I wasn't supposed to leave it. That hadn't ever happened, but I had enough food and bottled water to last me for a few days. I wasn't even allowed to go to the bathroom. I had to use a can. Father promised me that if, God forbid, anything happened to him, someone else — like Boruch — would come to get me. I didn't want to think about it, though.

Anyway, I wasn't so worried. Father was big and strong. When he was younger, he was a boxer. I was sure that he was the strongest person in the factory. And he had a pistol too. And he was handsome. Mother didn't marry him without good reason.

Still, as soon as he came home at night and whistled, I'd jump on him and hug him hard, so I guess I must have been worried all day without knowing it. He'd throw me in the air, even though I was big and heavy and not a baby anymore, and catch me and give me a kiss.

Father would sit down to rest when he came home and I would make him supper. Only dumb people think that boys can't cook or should be ashamed to. Even Boruch once told me that the best chefs in the world are men. I told him that I made father tea, and omelets and boiled potatoes for us both.

"Why don't you invite me for dinner some time?" Boruch said.

So I did. And he really came. He brought some salami and a different bread than the kind we got at the factory. I made tea and potatoes but we were out of eggs, so I couldn't show him how I flipped an omelet. He believed me that I could, though, because father swore to it. The one thing we didn't do was put Snow on the table as usual. He squeaked in his box and I felt sorry for him. But I guess we had to think of our guest first.

After the meal, father and Boruch talked about the war. They took out a large map and argued about the price the Germans were already paying on the Russian front, pointing with their fingers and making marks with a pencil. Then they played chess. They were both so tired that they ended the game before either of them had won. Which was just as well with me, because that way I didn't have to feel sorry for the loser. Sometimes they played so hard to win that you couldn't even talk to them; you'd think it was a war and not just some game. I guess it was the same as my wanting to beat father so badly at cards that I became angry when I lost.

If father wasn't too tired at night, he sat by my bed and we talked, just like we used to when I was little.

Once, when mother was still with us and I was much

smaller, I remember that we had a big fight. We must have been talking about mother or something, and then father asked me what I thought I'd be like if he had married another woman. Well, I said, I'd be a little different, because I'd have a mother with another husband and a father with another wife. At first I didn't even notice that I was talking about two different children and that I'd split myself into halves. I didn't realize that couldn't be. It took awhile for me to see that father's point was that I wouldn't have been born at all. If the two of them hadn't met and had me exactly when they did, I wouldn't even exist. That's what made us fight. I wouldn't talk to him at night anymore until he promised never to ask me that question again.

Today it doesn't make me angry, although I still can't explain myself or prove it any better than I could then. I guess that's impossible. I just know that whatever happened, I would exist anyway. I might have different parents and I certainly wouldn't look the same, but I'd still be me. Maybe not now. Maybe in a different time. Let's say after the war. I wouldn't mind so much being born when all this was over.

There was one thing I agreed with, though. That was when mother broke in to say that I could have been born a girl. She was right, and I didn't think it contradicted anything I'd said. It just made me laugh to think about it.

Mother took my side in that argument. She told father he was needling me. She said that if that's how I felt, then it must be right for me. No one could ever prove otherwise. And if father felt the way he did, that must be right for him. You couldn't argue about such things. You could only say how you felt.

Maybe that's why I took mother's side when it came to Zionism. Father didn't agree with her there. Before the war he wouldn't hear of going to Palestine. He felt at home in Poland. Mother didn't.

"You're oversensitive," he used to say to her. "Whenever anyone sticks out his tongue, you're sure that it's aimed at you. So what if you're Jewish? Protestants and Moslems get called names too."

Mother said it wasn't the same, and they fought. It went on and on, even when it no longer mattered and we couldn't go to Palestine anyway.

I don't remember exactly how mother used to answer him. It was awfully complicated, one of those arguments that never ends. Sometimes they really went at it seriously and sometimes they just joked. For instance, father would say: "Do you know what a Zionist is? It's a rich Jew who ships a poor Jew off to Palestine."

The first time it made mother laugh. Not me. I had to have it explained to me. But afterward, when father told the same joke over and over, it made mother mad.

Father liked to say that we were all human beings. It didn't matter what color your skin was, how long your nose was, or by what name you called God. So what difference did it make where you lived, here or in Honolulu? This made sense to me. But mother would sigh and say: "If only you were right."

One thing she said stuck in my memory, the example of the tree: "It may make no difference whether you were born a Chinese or an African or an Indian, but once you've been born, you can't deny your roots. When you dig up a tree's roots, it dies." She went on. "People don't die when they deny their past, but they can't be themselves. They grow up sad and twisted, and so do their children."

Father disagreed. He said that by the second or third generation you could forget. But he admitted that Jews had deep roots that went way back, even if they became Christians. Did father want to become a Christian, too? I don't think so. That would have been a coward's way out, and he certainly wasn't a coward. Anyway, that's why mother wanted to go to Palestine. Polish society denied her roots.

I sided with mother only because she sided with me. I wasn't really sure that she was right. Today, though, I know she was.

3

We're Caught, Old Boruch Has a Plan

It all happened so suddenly. No one was ready for it. There were no advance rumors and none of the Polish foremen even dropped a hint. Maybe they didn't know either. That morning everyone came to work as usual. I was with Boruch in the storeroom. Snow stayed home. Luckily, I'd left his box open, because he cried if he had to sit in it all day. Father had promised me that the house was airtight and that there was no way for him to get out.

"Suppose he gnaws a hole somewhere?"

"We'll be back before he has time to."

Even before the Poles were told to leave, the factory was surrounded by Polish and Jewish policemen and German soldiers. There were soldiers in black uniforms, too, who were either Lithuanians or Ukranians — I couldn't tell which.

Everyone began running around. It didn't take long to see that I wasn't the only one hiding in the factory during work hours. There were other children too. Nobody knew what to do. Should we try to escape? If you looked out the window escape didn't seem possible, but there was a secret passage that led to the roof, and from there, up the street through empty apartments and lofts. Before we could make up our minds to reach home by it, though, and hide in the ceiling or bunker, shots rang out. Someone had ratted and given the passage away. Who had been shot? I was glad that I was here with father and not by myself in the hideout.

My greatest fear had always been that father would be caught somewhere and I would be left all alone in the ceiling or down in the bunker. Of course, he had promised that he'd find a way to get back to me in a day or two. But what if he couldn't? Mother had said she'd be right back too.

Father came running to the storeroom.

"It's a selection," he said.

I knew what that meant. Everyone was rounded up in the yard, and then one by one you went out through a gate where the German factory owner and his Polish partner would be standing with policemen. It was they who decided who stayed in the ghetto to work and who was transported. Naturally, children and old people didn't stand a chance. Neither did anyone who had a child with him.

Boruch said right away that he wasn't going. He would hide. Afterward he would manage to get a valid work permit. He had connections with the Polish partner, because he had worked for him as a foreman before the war. That's how he had gotten this job on which his life depended.

Sometimes, when I was alone in the hideout, I'd think about what it would be like to be someone on whom others' lives depended. I'd think, for instance, that if it were up to me, I'd decide to save anyone who had a big space between his front teeth, because I had one myself. But father and Boruch didn't have spaces. It would have to be something else, then, like blue eyes. Only I'd also have the right to save three people who had brown eyes. One, of course, would be mother. Father and Boruch were no problem. All the rest of the brown-eyed people would have to pass before me. Next I'd pick little Yossi, who was the nicest of the Gryns. But that was ridiculous. How could I pick one child out of a whole family? I'd have to give myself the right to save ten lives. In the end, I'd just get depressed, maybe because it was taking father so long to get home.

What made the Polish partner give Boruch a job he was too old for? I guess it was their being old friends. Although while Boruch really was old, he was still strong and healthy enough to work well.

He crawled in among the bales of rope where I was hiding and waited for father to decide what to do. Father was thinking. He knew that they would take me, even though that meant splitting us up. Trying to resist would only make things worse, so he made up his mind to hide too. The three of us crawled deeper into the rope and father dragged a big, heavy bale of it after us to cover our tracks.

We heard whistles being blown and policemen running upstairs to seal off the roof. Then we heard footsteps going down to the yard. A boy cried out for his mother. The Jewish policemen shouted, "Everyone downstairs!" And then in German, *"Alle runter gehen!"*

They began a floor-to-floor search for those still hiding. Then they reached the storeroom, and we could hear them talking. We held our breaths and I hugged father hard, trying to feel the pistol. It was still there.

They began to move the bales of rope. How did they know? Someone must have ratted. Maybe someone who thought it would save him. Rats were even worse than Germans. You knew the Germans couldn't be trusted. They didn't try to hide that they were murderers. They even wore skull patches on their uniforms. But a rat smiled and talked to you like a friend and then went and squealed behind your back. He thought he'd gain time for himself. Like the Germans, who thought they'd win the war — though in the end they'd pay for what they had done. The rats would pay too. Only sooner. That's what Boruch said, and he knew. Because the Germans would kill the rats themselves, even before they lost the war. No rat would get away from them.

I had a funny thought when they caught us. It was, "What luck that Snow is at home." As though he were a Jew too, and would have been beaten and dragged out to the yard for selection like the rest of us.

Boruch was kicked in the rear. A policeman kicked father too. Father wheeled around and the policeman backed off. Not that father actually threatened him. But after that they were more polite and even left Boruch alone.

We were among the last to be brought down to the yard before the selection began, at which point father and Boruch began to fight over me. It wasn't exactly a fight; it was a disagreement. But it was like a fight because each was so sure he was right. And there was hardly any time left to decide. Boruch's plan was for father to go ahead through the gate without me. Of course, he would be sent to the right. Boruch and I would follow later. We would be sent to the left. Selections had nothing to do with being good or bad. That was only in Heaven.

"Do you know that ruined building on our street?" whispered Boruch. "Number seventy-eight. I'll hide him there and you'll get him afterward."

That was the house that had been bombed out at the beginning of the war. I knew where it was. So did father.

"How will you hide him?"

"Leave that to me," whispered Boruch.

"If someone has to lay down his life to save my son, that someone will be me!"

"If you're so anxious to die for him, go right ahead," laughed Boruch.

It wasn't a real laugh, though. It was a make-believe one. I knew how his real laugh sounded. And this wasn't the same. But then he said that father mustn't die for me, because I needed a father who was alive. And would go on needing one for many years to come, even when the war was over.

Father didn't want to listen, though. He had another plan — although, it wasn't really a plan. Father said he would go with me. Of course, we'd be sent to the left with Boruch. And then somewhere we'd make a run for it. Maybe on the way to the train. Or else in the depot itself. Or we might even jump from one of the cars. Father had a hammer and a metal-cutting saw tucked into his belt beneath his jacket, and on our way out of the storeroom, I had seen him slip pliers into his pocket. The policeman who kicked him had seen him too. Father and Boruch were worried that he might rat. They had talked about it in whispers even before they fought over me.

"You'll go first," Boruch insisted. "Usually the ones not taken get sent home. At least that's what happened the last time. From there you'll reach Alex by the lofts."

"How can I?" asked father. "He'll be three blocks away."

"So what? You'll come down to cross at the corners. You're just being stubborn. Listen to what an old man has to tell you!"

"I can't bear the thought of you dying for my son," said father.

"Are you serious? Why, it's a golden opportunity to die for something! All along I've kept wondering how I could do some good when I die. And here's a chance to save someone I love! You should be ashamed of yourself, trying to keep me from doing the one thing I really want to do."

Father laughed. So did Boruch. They hugged each other. Then father bent down to reassure me. "Don't be afraid, Alex. Everything will be all right."

The argument would have ended here anyway, because the Germans decided to make it easy for us. There was to be no selection. The Polish partner came up and whispered in Boruch's ear, "This time it's all of you."

That worried me. There would be no way to go back and get Snow. I tried to tell myself that he would manage. He'd have plenty of time to gnaw his way out. And anyway, the apartment was big enough for a little thing like himself. He was sure to get into the cupboard somehow.

Just then the policeman who saw father take the pliers whispered something to one of the Germans. The German smiled and grabbed father, and at the same time, Boruch yanked me through the gate. There really was no selection. Outside in the street everyone stood in one large group. Boruch lifted me on his shoulders and, over the heads of the crowd, I saw father still at the gate. He handed the German

the pliers. The German slapped him in the face. He handed
him the hammer. Another slap. Then he said something
that made the German laugh. It's not always a good sign
when a German laughs. But this German didn't hit father
again.

They began to search him and found the saw. I knew
that they would kill him on the spot if they found the pistol
too. My heart pounded so hard that I thought I was going
to choke. But they didn't find it — though I saw them
search him *all* over. Then they ordered everyone in the
street to line up by threes. Father hadn't joined us yet and
there was still a crowd in the yard. They must have decided
to bring us to the depot in two groups, and ours was the
first.

"Father!" I began to shout.

But Boruch gripped my arm hard and told me to be
quiet. Father stayed with the second group.

We started out. The whole way Boruch kept coaching
me about what I would have to do. As soon as we reached
78 Bird Street I would make a dash for the front gate by
myself. I knew the house. It was full of windows without
glass. There was nothing left inside it either, just smashed
walls with bits of floor hanging from them and pipes sticking up in the air. Boruch would give me a push when the
time came. He promised that father would follow me. Or
else that he would slip away and join me later, in two or
three days at the most. At any rate, I had to stay put as long
as I could. Even if it took a whole month. Even if it took a
whole year.

"You're a bright boy," he said. "You'll manage. If they
mean to kill us all, the children have the worst odds. It's no

easy job to throw a child from a moving train, especially since they took the tools from your father. If you can't saw a hole near the floor, you have to jump from the window near the ceiling."

Then he told me something that I already knew: In the ruined house there was a small opening that led down to a cellar. It was so narrow that only a child could squeeze through it.

"My father had something else with him," I whispered.

"I know," Boruch said. "We saw that the policeman noticed him taking the pliers. I have it."

"But how will he get it back?" I asked, worried.

"You'll give it to him," said Boruch, hanging his knapsack on my shoulder.

I didn't say anything.

"Do you know what to do now, Alex?"

I nodded.

"Run straight to the opening and work your way as far into it as you can. Don't be afraid. You've got a flashlight in the knapsack."

Boruch must have planned my escape long ahead of time. But I only thought of that later; right now my mind was a blank. He kept giving me last-minute advice. How to get along. How to find food. I didn't hear a thing, though. All I could think of was father being hit by the German at the gate and the pistol in Boruch's knapsack on my shoulder. Just then he gave me a shove. I took off as fast as I could. I always was a good runner. A policeman ran after me. Boruch ran after him. Suddenly the policeman fell. I'll never know for sure, but I think that Boruch must have tripped him. Then I heard a scream of pain. It wasn't Boruch. I was already through the front gate and inside the ruined house, making straight for the hole in the wall, when I heard shots in the street. I squeezed through the narrow opening. When we boys played hide-and-seek here before the transports began, we never went any farther than where I was. The deepest we got into the cellar was right here, where there still was some light. The darkness inside was too scary. We were sure there were ghosts in there.

I heard people chasing me. There was a sound of falling bricks and of voices shouting in German: "He's here!" "No, he's over there!"

I forced myself to grope carefully down a few steps that were part of a corridor. I hadn't gone very far, though, when I sat down. I was awfully frightened. And then I remembered that I had the pistol. I opened the knapsack and felt for it with shaky fingers. A bottle of water. Some bread. The flashlight. I left them where they were. Something soft wrapped in paper, jam or margarine. Finally, I felt the leather strap and the sling of the pistol. I pulled it from the knapsack, opened my coat, and hung it around my neck. Then I changed my mind, took it from its sling, and tried putting it in my pocket. It was too big, so I made a hole in the pocket with my penknife and pushed the barrel into it. Now the gun fit. I felt pleased with myself. Doing something had calmed me, even though they were still very near, right outside the opening. Suppose they came in after me, though? I decided to try an experiment and stood up. As I reached for the pistol I heard father say, just as he had in our lessons, "What counts most is the element of surprise. They'll never guess that you're armed. Take your time. You'll be more accurate from close up. If one is behind the other, you can thread them both with one shot."

The word *thread* made me laugh. As though they were a

bunch of beads. Did mother know about the pistol? I was sure she wouldn't have laughed. She never thought such things were funny. She hated all the war books that father and I loved. Even Sinkiewicz's *By Fire and Sword,* which is the greatest book of all time. She said it was too cruel, but that's just what made it so exciting.

I drew the pistol and cocked it quietly. I aimed it straight ahead of me. If they came for me now, they'd have the light at their backs and I'd see them outlined against it. That gave me an advantage. And then I remembered that unless the hole was widened they couldn't even fit through it.

They began shooting up at the floors above them. What were they aiming at? Didn't they know that I was down here?

And then I couldn't hear them anymore. I uncocked the pistol and put it back in my pocket, first wrapping it in my handkerchief to keep it clean. I drank a little water from the bottle and switched on the flashlight. It had a strong beam. I switched it off again. I would need it at night and mustn't waste the batteries. I would need it to check out the cellar too: Maybe I'd find a good hiding place there. I thought of Snow. What was he doing now? And then I heard shouts and lots of footsteps far away in the street. The second group, with father in it. I wanted to run out to him. He didn't even have his gun. Or had he already gotten away? He might not be there at all, and I would be caught right off. Boruch had told me that if I didn't stay put father would never find me. "Never" was awfully scary to think about. Like dying. "No matter if it takes a week, a month, or even a whole year." The tread of footsteps and the shouts were growing fainter. And then they were gone. I stayed put.

I returned to my corner and fell asleep with my head on Boruch's knapsack. I had a dream about him. In it he came and talked to me, and I couldn't understand how he had managed to squeeze through the opening.

It was dark when I awoke. Had someone sealed the opening? I felt panic. Slowly I crept up to it. No, it was just night outside. And so quiet. The only sounds of life came from the rear of the building, over on the Polish side.

4

The Ruined House

For as long as we'd been living in the ghetto, we children from Bird Street had gone to Number 78 to play hide-and-seek and all kinds of "secret" war games. Our parents had strictly forbidden us to enter the building because of the bricks that kept tumbling down in it. Father even said that a whole wall might suddenly collapse on us. And yet we couldn't keep ourselves away from the mysterious cellar with its storage rooms full of ghosts, from the jagged walls of the apartments on the bottom floors, and from the stairs that seemed to hang in midair. There wasn't a better place to play anywhere.

Part of the house must have burned down when it was bombed and part must have fallen down later. The houses next to it hadn't been damaged at all, and its own front and rear walls were still in place too. That is, neither reached solidly all the way up to where the roof once was, but both of them, leaning here and there on some inner wall or pipe, still stood with their gaping, sooty windows that opened in on nothing like two big frightening stage sets. The front of the house and its gate faced our street in the ghetto, while the back looked out on the Christian section of town.

The view from Number 78 was as irresistible as the house itself. It wasn't easy to get to the only rear window that could be reached by an unsupported flight of stairs, which had to be climbed one child at a time because it couldn't take any more weight. The window was on the second floor. Above it were four more windows in a row. Altogether the house had once had six floors, and of course there was the cellar below.

The entire length of the street behind the house was divided by a high brick wall that was topped by broken glass. Beyond it you could see the houses on the Polish side. They were so close that you could almost reach out and touch them, but they belonged to a different world. It was a world that we too had once lived in without really appreciating it. It had never occurred to us then that being able to walk down any street we pleased was a special privilege. Or to take a trolley out of town. Or even to go to the big public park and throw breadcrumbs to the swans and run around. Of course, before the transports began there were stores and things to do in the ghetto too. There was an empty lot to play football in and we had our ruined house to play in. But there was always the border beyond — the line you couldn't cross. It was like being in a prison that happened to be slightly larger than most. Besides which, over there, in the Polish stores, there was a lot more food and it cost a lot less. True, anything fancy was expensive there, too, but not as expensive as in the ghetto. You could always buy milk and bread. Even if sometimes there weren't any eggs, there was always bread. The milk might have some water in it, but a little water never hurt anyone. At least there people didn't die of hunger every night and get their corpses thrown into the street.

One by one we'd climb up to the window for a look. Until this big bully who lived on the other side began to throw stones at us. At first we wanted to throw them back. We had plenty of them. But in the end we decided to play it safe, because they might brick up the window if we threw junk out of it onto their side of the wall. If we hadn't had to play it safe, I know I could have easily knocked his brains out.

He wasn't German, but the Poles hated us too. Father said that was because of what they learned at home and in school and in church. They were told that the Jews crucified Jesus, and that they were all cheats and thieves and loan sharks. Father said that there were Polish cheats and thieves and loan sharks, too, and even murderers. At least we Jews didn't murder and didn't get drunk all the time. But if someone is a stranger, or if you think he is, it's easy to hate him. If there's no work, for instance, the unemployed can always say: "The Jews took all the jobs! Send them to Palestine!"

The stores on the Polish side were hidden by the wall. Sometimes we looked longingly up at the windows above us, because we could have seen so much more from them. There was just no way of reaching them, though.

On the third and fourth floors, hanging in space, were broken-off sections of floor. Once, one of us pointed out that you could tell by the white tiles and the remains of a cupboard on the wall that there had been kitchens there. In fact, you could tell that our second-floor window had belonged to a kitchen too; beneath the window was what was left of a larder, the metal air vent of which faced the Polish side.

Lots of sparrows and other birds were always landing on

the fourth floor and flapping around it as though there were food there. Once I took my life in my hands and climbed up some ruins across from it until I could see its wrecked kitchen. I wasn't high enough to see the floor itself but attached to the wall above it — I could hardly believe my eyes! — was a sink with a dripping faucet. The birds were coming to drink from it. Yet how was that possible? Perhaps the water main ran into the ghetto from the Polish side. On the third floor there was also a sink that was covered with chipped plaster and brick and bits of broken floorboard. And there were larders on both these floors, too, still with their doors on. I could make them out clearly.

Our street didn't get its name from those birds, but mother once told me how it did. Once upon a time, before there were automobiles, there was an avenue of trees in the middle of the street beneath whose branches the horse-drawn carriages passed back and forth. It was so long ago that even mother didn't remember them. Only grandmother did. And she said that those trees were bursting with birds. Thousands and thousands of them. That's why they called the street Bird Street. Maybe the birds in our ruined house were the great-grandchildren of the great-great-grandchildren of those same birds, because, for a bird, a generation isn't long.

Boruch once told me that a human generation was forty years.

"But you're already old when you're twenty," I said. He just laughed. The way he looked at it, a man of fifty or even fifty-five was still young. "When you get to be fifty yourself," he said, "you'll see that I'm right."

That was hard to believe, though. Poor Snow would be old when he was three. How long is a generation for a mouse? According to the encyclopedia, one mouse can give birth eight times in a single year. Go figure that one out!

I could never have told my parents about the birds and the leaky faucet. They would have known right away that I had disobeyed them. Not only that. No sooner had I climbed down again than the entire wall I had been on toppled all at once and filled the building with a great cloud of dust. We ran outside coughing and one boy said to me, "You sure are lucky, Alex."

I sure was. And I would have given anything to be able to tell father and mother about it. In fact, father had often said to me, "Alex, you were born lucky." And mother had an explanation for it: I was born with a "hat on," and anyone born with a "hat on" was supposed to have good luck. What that really meant, mother said, was that some babies were born with part of the sac that enclosed them in the womb still over their heads. It was just a superstition, but lots of superstitions proved true.

Boruch agreed with her.

The three of them were my teachers. Not that I didn't have teachers in school, even in the ghetto, but all the important things I knew I'd learned from mother, father, and Boruch.

"Whenever you pick a hiding place, always make sure that it has an emergency exit." That Boruch taught me.

"What counts most is the element of surprise. Be sure to take your time . . ." That father taught me.

"If you relate to people with trust and human kindness, they will always help you." That mother taught me.

When father heard that, though, he said:

legal now for factory workers to keep children. It
ays been. At first it was allowed. Then, one day,
:ement was made that it wasn't. Panic set in. Fa-
d to send me to Polish friends of his in the coun-
other refused to let me go. She was afraid of my
ir away by myself, with no one to look after me.
:n we decided to make the hideout in the ceiling,
the bunker with the Gryns.

rmans left the workers alone because they needed
so we thought. Father was sure of it. It's logical,
ut Boruch said they didn't always act logically.
e German factory boss simply wanted to make
, just as brushes were made in the brush factory
it Miller's sock works. The boss's Polish partner,
riend, certainly didn't want to close down. He had
whole factory before the war.

id the Germans need all that rope for? Once I
er and mother if it was to tie up Russian prison-
laughed.

ather said. "It's to hang themselves with."
ises that I passed were still full of whatever their
d left behind. No one understood why the Ger-
i't already stripped them bare, as they were sup-
iave done elsewhere. Maybe it was a good sign;
was a bad one. Father said that they had their
on the Russian front. That was just a joke,
made Boruch laugh. He said that they were still
ut Ghetto B and would get to us in good time.
was where the rich Jews had lived. No one was
ir street. Not many people had had good furni-
be that's why the Germans were in no hurry.
ht of our chairs. They weren't the most beautiful

"Be kind but trust only yourself." Now I felt confused.

"It depends on the situation," said mother. "An intelligent person knows when to follow one rule and when to follow the other. But I wasn't thinking so much of the specific way one should behave. I was thinking of the feelings that one should have in one's heart. And the heart should have kindness and love in it. That doesn't mean you always have to act on them. Certainly not when you're facing a murderer with a skull patch on his uniform."

Father was silent for a while and then said, "Yes, Alex, that's so."

And while I'm on the subject of luck. Once, when the Germans were bombing us at the beginning of the war, I happened to be in the street. Suddenly there was an air-raid alert. A strange man tried dragging me after him into his house. I stood by the front gate for a second and then all at once I turned and ran home.

"Hey, come back!" he shouted. "Come on back!"

He was afraid that I would be hit by a piece of shrapnel or even by a whole bomb. Just then there was a loud boom and dust and stones went flying in all directions. I threw myself face down in the street by the sidewalk, just as father had taught me to do. As soon as the dust and the noise had died down, even before the all-clear, I stood up and looked back. I couldn't believe what I saw. The whole front of the man's house had disappeared from sight. Even the gate was gone. There was nothing left but a smoking pile of rubble. Policemen and rescue squads came running to dig for survivors.

Sometimes I thought of my luck as an angel or some kind of good spirit, or as some force that wanted to keep me alive. But father didn't believe in blind fate. He used to tell me, "You can be the master of your fate, Alex."

Boruch, on the other hand, liked to say, "It's all in the cards. No one can escape his destiny, for good or for bad."

I wondered whether it was somehow already decided what would happen to everyone. I doubted it. Because if it was, why bother doing anything? Maybe fate was more like a prediction: If you did such-and-such, then such-and-such would happen, and if you didn't, it wouldn't. Maybe that much was in the cards. Who could know?

And maybe fate wasn't just for human beings, either. Maybe if Snow could get into our cupboard, he was fated to live. A mouse could live for three years. I read that in some book. Or else he might not have to gnaw his way into it, because I might be fated to go get him. And if that was in the cards, the card must have my name on it: Alex.

Since the day mother didn't come back, I'd started to think that she was my lucky charm. I mean that she was somewhere near me and watching over me. Sometimes, out of the corner of my eye, I even thought I saw her shadow flitting by.

My First V
an

I decided to get Snow. I took the
and left everything else inside the c
until evening. First, though, I bu
around it, on top of which I put a s
mice out, although I hadn't hear
mice preferred the cellars of hous
couldn't say I blamed them.

After giving it a lot of thought, I
sling. Then I made a belt for it fr
der straps and tied it around my w
would have liked to carry it under r
didn't fit there. Last of all I made
so that I could draw it straight fror

The moon had risen and the st
houses were all dark. It wasn't beca
over a week they had been empty, e
left behind in them. The Germans
street, and all of Ghetto C in whic
but the factory workers and peopl
me.

It was
hadn't al
an annou
ther wan
try. But
being so
That's w
and later
The C
them. O
he said.
Maybe
more ro
and sock
Boruch'
owned t
What
asked fa
ers. Th
"No,
The
tenants
mans h
posed t
maybe
hands
though
cleanin
Ghetto
rich on
ture. M
I th

in the world, but they were nice just the same. Especially after father and I had repainted them a light blue. Who would sit on them in Germany? Once I asked Boruch that, and he said, "What do you care who sits on them? Let them sit all they want, till an American or British bomb hits them!"

I felt bad for those chairs. And I felt even worse for my toys. My books, at least, the Germans couldn't read. They were all in Polish.

I'd better explain about the ghettos. There were three of them. Ghetto B was cleared early on. Ghetto C, our ghetto, had the war factories. And in Ghetto A, which was very big and crowded, the evacuation had begun and then stopped. They'd get back to it soon enough, Boruch promised. Meanwhile a whole lot of people still lived there. It had lots of streets and alleys, and lots of cellars and lofts beneath roofs. And it had bunkers, deep underground, with enough water and food for a year. And of course it had lots of stinking rats. But it also had members of Zionist groups like mother's, and lots of workingmen and all kinds of tough characters. It was the young people, father predicted, who would rise in revolt in the end.

"Something like what happened in the Warsaw ghetto," he said. "Maybe it won't last as long here. Just for a few days. But still, a real uprising."

"What are they waiting for?" asked Boruch.

"They can't begin as long as there are so many families with children still around. And maybe they don't have the weapons yet. There's no point in starting unless they can really hurt the Germans and keep it up for at least three days."

I walked on the dark side of the street, away from the

moonlight, trying to hug the walls of the houses as closely as I could. "Stop to listen now and then," father had told me. "Look around you and behind you. Danger doesn't only strike from the front." He taught me things like that when we sneaked out together during night curfews to buy bread from smugglers. We always took a different way back, entering at the rear of the building through a window whose bars had been sawed. Father would whistle, and Boruch would whistle back from inside.

It was hard to stick close to the houses. All kinds of junk, broken furniture, and things that I couldn't make out in the dark were scattered along the sidewalk, especially in the doorways. I had to make a detour around each of these piles, and each time I did, I thought I saw a German staring out at me. Once I really did see the eyes of a cat, and for the first time in my life I actually felt the hair stand up on my head. Until then I'd thought it was just something made up for scary books.

Finally, I left the sidewalk and walked in the street, even though that made me more visible. At least I could walk faster that way and not come so near the spooky shapes.

To tell the truth, I don't know which frightened me more, Germans or ghosts. I knew that no German would go to the trouble of hiding in all that junk just to catch some Jew who shouldn't be out at night. The Germans liked coming in broad daylight, Boruch said, after a nice big breakfast. And when they came, they brought help — all kinds of policemen to do their dirty work. The fact was that I think I was more scared of ghosts, even if it should have been the other way around.

Suddenly a door in a house that I was passing slammed

shut with a really loud bang. It made such a sound in the quiet street that I thought it must be a gunshot. A few seconds later I heard something creak and then another loud bang. But it was just an open door swinging back and forth in a draft.

All the way to our house noises like that kept making me freeze in my tracks. All kinds of squeaky, creaky windows and doors. Once a handful of feathers from a torn pillow or quilt blew spookily out of a doorway without a sound and made me jump against a wall. I tried talking to myself, reasoning with myself. But the fact that I knew these were things that wouldn't scare me in the daytime didn't make me feel any better.

Besides furniture and household goods, the sidewalks were littered with open or torn suitcases that had been left because they were too heavy to carry. Maybe their owners had remembered at the last moment to take something valuable from them, or maybe the looters had gotten to them.

In the end I quit worrying and stopping all the time. I took off my shoes, held them in one hand, and ran the rest of the way in my stocking feet. I knew the way well. The gate was locked of course. I went around to the back, shinnied up the wall, and gave the sawed-through window a push. It creaked open like it always did. I crawled through it, jumped down into the courtyard, and crossed it without making a sound. There was no one there, although for a moment I thought I heard a noise. Like of something on the roof. Could somebody be up there? What had happened to the Gryns? Was that them? I climbed the stairs. The front door of the apartment was open. I ran inside as if father were waiting for me. But of course he wasn't. We had arranged to meet in Number 78. I did hear Snow squeak, though. If he hadn't been so small I would have given him a big hug. I'll bet he was one happy mouse to be picked up and put in my coat pocket.

I was worried by the thought that I should have left some sign for father in Number 78, and I turned to head back. Just then, though, it occurred to me that I should take a few things with me — my pillow and blanket, for instance, and some food. I went to the cupboard, but it was open and empty. Someone had cleaned it out, I thought angrily. Maybe someone else who had decided to hide here and didn't know that father and I were coming back.

We had stockpiled some food in the hideout in the ceiling too. I climbed up to it. Again the same story. Someone had been there before me and taken it all. Someone, I was sure, who knew the place well. Could it have been father? The hideout was well concealed. Except for the two of us and Boruch, no one but the Gryns knew about it. And about the bunker. I went to the bathroom and tried moving the toilet that hid the bunker's entrance, but it wouldn't budge. As though it had been made fast from below. I pulled as hard as I could. Nothing gave. I tapped on the floor and whispered: "Pan Gryn! Pani Gryn! Tsippora! Avrom! Yossi!"

No one answered. I remembered our secret signal and knocked once and then twice. Still no answer. I banged as hard as I could and shouted: "Pan Gryn!"

They let me in and turned on me in a fury.

"What are you shouting for? Do you want to bring the whole German army here? And all the informers? What kind of idiot are you?"

That was an insult. I climbed down and Gryn closed the

trap door. Father wasn't there. But they had no right to talk to me like that. When grown-ups call you names it's not like when children do. It's a lot more insulting. And it was all his own fault.

"Why didn't you answer?" I shot back.

"We answered immediately," he said. "The nerve of you!"

He raised his hand to hit me. I retreated.

"Stop it, Mietek," said his wife. "Come, sit down, Alex. Where is your father?"

"He was in the second group," I said.

"And you came back without him?"

"I didn't come back. I never went anywhere."

"But where were you? You certainly weren't here . . ."

"Was it you who took all our food?"

"No," said Gryn.

I knew that he was lying. I looked at Tsippora and at little Yossi, who hid his face in his mother's dress. Avrom climbed up to the top bunk and covered himself with a blanket.

"You took the food that was in the ceiling too," I said. I wasn't afraid of him. Let him try to kill me. Let his children see what kind of a father they had.

"We didn't take anything," Pani Gryn said too sweetly.

Boruch always called them *Galitsiyaners,* the lowest of the low. Maybe this was what he meant. What could I do, though? There were five of them, two of them adults. And Avrom and Tsippora were bigger than me, too. But there was food in the bunker that father and Pan Gryn had stored together so that we could hold out for months. They couldn't pretend that there wasn't.

"All right," I said. "I want our share of the food. I'll bring a sack and take as much as I can. Then I'll come back for more."

Pan Gryn jumped up like a man with a snake in his pants and looked as though he were going to brain me. But his wife grabbed hold of him and made him sit down.

"Be quiet," she said to him. "Let me talk to the boy."

She turned to me and said in the same sugary voice, "Look, Alex, there are a few things that you have to understand. The first is that you can't come and go here as you please. You're a big boy and you know that you'll give us away. You know that there are informers everywhere. I only hope that no one saw you come here or heard your stupid shouts."

"You should have let me in when I —"

She didn't let me finish. "That doesn't matter. Now listen to me carefully, Alex. If you leave now, you'll have to promise never to come back. That's the first thing."

"But —" I began. I wanted to say that it was our bunker. Our food.

"Fine, I know all that. Listen to me now."

I listened.

"You can stay here with us for as long as you like and we'll share our food with you. Is that clear?"

"Yes, Pani," I answered politely.

"Good. You can lie down now on one of the bunks and Tsippora will give you something to eat when you're hungry. We have to watch ourselves, though, because no one knows how much longer we'll be here. The war is nowhere near ending."

"I can't stay here," I said.

"I'll say you can't!" snarled Pan Gryn.

His wife didn't answer him this time. Yossi, Tsippora, and Avrom stared at me in disbelief.

"I have to go back to . . . to wait for my father," I said.

"Where is that?" asked Pan and Pani Gryn in one breath.

"It's — ," I caught myself in the nick of time.

"Don't you trust us? Why don't you tell us? Is your father there now? Or maybe somebody else is? Who sent you here?"

The questions came all at once.

"No," I said. "No one sent me. I'm there by myself. I'm waiting for my father."

"Then what made you come here?" asked Pan Gryn.

"To get Snow."

"Snow?" asked the Gryns.

"His pet mouse," said Yossi.

They all burst out laughing except for Pan Gryn. I felt mortified. Thank God that Snow was at least keeping still in my pocket.

"I wanted some food and there wasn't any left. So I came down here to take our share of it. I'll carry it all upstairs and come back for more when I need it. I won't come down here again or even knock."

"That's out of the question," said Pan Gryn.

He and his wife went off to whisper in a corner. I could tell that they were quarreling. Finally Pani Gryn came back to me and said in a harsh voice, "You can stay with us or you can go, but you're not taking any food with you."

"Why not?"

"It will just go to waste," said Pan Gryn. "You'll be caught in a day or two and never get to eat it."

"Stay here," whispered Yossi.

"I can't," I said, on the verge of tears. "I'm waiting for my father, and . . ."

"Your father will come to look for you here too," Avrom said.

He was right. That made sense. I should stay with them. I looked at them. Yossi looked back at me eagerly. Tsippora and Avrom weren't really that bad. But I knew I had to go. I had to get back to the ruined house. I tried to think. Boruch knew about our bunker, and he hadn't said anything about staying in it if father didn't come the first night. He had said, "Wait in Number Seventy-eight. Even if it takes a week, a month, or a whole year."

That's what he had said. And that's what I had to do.

Pani Gryn gave me three cans of evaporated milk. I couldn't prove anything, but it was the same brand that had been in our cupboard. She handed me some crackers and a jar of jam.

"That's it," she said.

"Stay with us, Alex," whispered Yossi again.

"Shut up," said Pan Gryn severely. "Mind your own business."

Even if they had paid me, I wouldn't have stayed there without father. Yet they had always seemed so nice to us whenever they dropped by our room to chat. Maybe rats were like that. Nice as long as it suited them. Until one day you saw what they were really like.

I went back upstairs and wrapped my blanket and my pillow in a thin bedspread. I added a few books, the food they had given me, a sheet, a towel, some underwear, and spare clothes. It was like packing for summer camp. I thought awhile and decided to take candles and matches, too. And father's pocket flashlight; now I had two. A fork, a tablespoon, a teaspoon, and a knife, and another set for father. I was about to leave when I remembered our family album and added it to the pile. I didn't want our photographs to be kicked around in the street some day like others I had seen.

I might never have noticed them on the ground if mother hadn't pointed them out. They were photographs, she explained, of people who had once been happy. Pictures of a wedding, for instance. Or of someone's old parents. Or of a new baby. They were, mother said, like tracks left behind by the dead. And they were of no use to anyone.

I started out. It wasn't easy to squeeze my bundle through the window. I pushed the bars back into place behind me. Maybe I would have to return here some day. Now no one could see that they were sawed. Old Boruch had done a good job.

The sky had turned cloudy. It had begun to drizzle. Suddenly I remembered all sorts of other things that I should have taken and didn't. Why hadn't I at least slept there? Should I have stayed in the bunker after all, even though I couldn't stand the Gryns? But I didn't turn back.

The return trip took me less time. Maybe I wasn't as careful. I wasn't any less scared, though. I couldn't help being scared.

By the time I reached Number 78 it had begun to rain real hard. I had to unpack my bundle in front of the opening to the cellar, since I couldn't drag it through in one piece. The blanket had gotten slightly wet. So had the books. Well, they would dry.

I made a bed for myself inside the opening, but the

ground was hard, so I decided to sleep on my blanket. To-morrow, I told myself, I'd look for a mattress in one of the houses on the street. Maybe I'd find some food too. That wasn't likely, though. Food was something you either took with you or hid well. Mattresses were sure to be every-where.

I dreamed about father. He smiled at me. He was so close that I put out my arms to hug him. I couldn't reach him, though. The more I tried, the farther away he got, even though he stayed in one place. "Father!" I shouted. It didn't do any good. I tried running to him. I saw him clearly but my legs were too heavy to move. Yet all the time he had such a good, encouraging smile on his face, as if to say: "Hang on, Alex. I'll come."

Twice I woke up. The first time I didn't know where I was. I must have been woken by my dream. The second time I was woken by a thunderstorm. Water was dripping into the cellar nearby me. I felt the bedspread on top of me. It was dry. I hadn't slept like this in my clothes since the days we were bombed by the Germans.

6

Worthless Treasure

I woke up early to the chirping of the birds and peered out through the hole in the wall. It was a fine morning. The ruined house had an after-rain smell that I loved. Still, I was in no mood to venture out again. I turned around, took a flashlight, and set out to investigate the cellar. It was a cellar like any other, with storage rooms opening off a central corridor that only seemed more frightening than most because it curved around in a U. It was odd, but now that I had to, I explored it without thinking twice, while back in the days when we played here I didn't dare take two steps inside before all the boys went "hooooo" like a ghost and I ran right back out again. And yet even if there really were ghosts and they hid in places like this, why would they want to harm me? Like as not, they wanted to help. They certainly had to hate the Germans too.

The storage rooms were all open and empty. By the beam of the flashlight I made out the traces of coal and rotted sacks that had once held potatoes. At the end of the corridor, under the ceiling, was a small skylight that was blocked from outside by the fallen debris of the house. I made a note to myself to try to find a ladder and clear the rubble away. A hiding place should have an emergency exit.

I chose the storage room nearest the opening, cleaned it with the help of an old sack, and put all my things in it. If father called me, I would be sure to hear him from here. Deeper inside the cellar I hadn't heard a thing, neither the quiet of the empty ghetto nor the noise from the street on the Polish side of the wall. To avoid wasting candles or batteries, I decided to read only by the opening in daylight. And that way I would hear if anyone entered the building and would have time to hide farther back.

I spent that whole day in the cellar. Father didn't come. The next day I decided to look for a mattress in one of the neighboring houses. I walked as far as the front gate but was afraid to step into the street in broad daylight. And then I remembered that once we boys had discovered a secret passage that led through the wall of Number 78 into an apartment next door. It had been boarded up, but now the apartment would be empty and I could break through. And in fact, when I found it, the boards were no longer there. Perhaps the tenants had tried escaping through the passage when the Germans came for them.

I passed through a nearly bare apartment and came out its front door by the stairs. I stood for a moment in the hallway. There wasn't a sound. I tried the door of the apartment across from me. It opened. Everything was in place, as though whoever lived here had stepped out for a moment and intended to come right back. Except that it looked a little messy, with things thrown about here and there and lots of dust.

I went straight to the kitchen. There wasn't any food

there. But that didn't worry me. What I'd gotten from the Gryns would last at least a week and by then father would come. I went to the children's room and found lots of books. Some of them I'd already read and some I hadn't. I took a blanket and began to collect them in it. I found a toy chest too. For a while I actually forgot where I was and began to play with the toys. And then all of a sudden I heard footsteps. Someone was walking in one of the apartments upstairs. I froze and didn't move for a long time until the steps receded and were gone. Looters, I thought. If I didn't act fast, there would be nothing left for me.

I went through the other apartments in the building. They were all unlocked. The Germans had made a point of leaving doors open to make searching for fugitives easier. I looked in all the kitchens. The food had either been taken or carefully hidden away. I opened the closets. Men's and women's wardrobes. Sheets and towels. Underwear. Treasure troves of clothes. I began pulling things out and collecting them in a pile at the bottom of the stairs. It kept growing bigger. The one thing there wasn't much of was books. I guess the only one who read them was the child in the first apartment.

I spread blankets on the ground and filled them with my treasure. I found three men's suits in good condition and took them all, because I wasn't sure what father's size was. I found a large, warm man's overcoat. I tied everything in bundles and tried lifting them. They were awfully heavy. And what, I thought frantically, about all the other houses in the neighborhood? How could I possibly collect so much stuff by myself? Suddenly I realized what a dope I was and sat down on a pile of clothes. What did I want all this for?

What could I do with it? God only knew how long I'd have to wait for father in the cellar. And even if he came, we could never escape from the ghetto with bundles of clothes on our backs. Once, when there were still shops and shoppers, we could have sold everything for lots of money and food. But now?

I stood looking at the piles of things that had taken me half a day's hard work to collect and gave one of them a kick. It scattered all over the stairs.

I decided to make just one bundle of clothes. Into it went a few things that fit me, the suits for father, the coat, and some towels and sheets. I found a beat-up Polish army hat, the kind tough Polish kids liked to wear, and stuck it happily on my head. Then I filled a second blanket with books and dragged the two bundles to the entrance to the cellar, where I took them apart and carried in a few things at a time. Before it got dark I went back again and took a mattress. I picked a nice soft one. And then I made one last trip for a folding chair that I managed to fit through the opening too.

In the middle of the night I woke up and heard voices. They seemed to come from the house next door that I had been in during the day. It took me a long while to fall asleep again. But no one entered Number 78.

In the morning I went next door again. I entered quietly. Silence. This time I knew exactly what to look for: candles and food. That was all that I needed. Except for a good book, if I found one. The piles of clothing had disappeared. Looters must have come in the night and taken everything. Well, they were welcome to it. The same apartments that had still looked pretty neat the day before were now turned upside-down. Like after a pogrom. I felt for father's pistol in my pocket.

I climbed up to the loft beneath the roof. Father had once explained to me that it was often easy to get from one loft to another because the tenants had made passageways between them for use when the streets were dangerous or under curfew. He was right. I went from building to building, stopping each time to listen. In one of them I found a large breadknife, which I took. But there was no food anywhere. I found a carrying bag on the floor, emptied it, and stuffed it with bottles of water. Father might not come for a whole week and I'd better not leave my cellar too often. It was too bad that I couldn't reach the water where I was, up there on the bird floor.

Three more days went by. I read and ate the food that I had gotten from the Gryns. It was beginning to run low. No one entered the ruin and there was no sign of father. It had been a whole week now. I began to worry. What next? Boruch had told me, "Wait . . . Even if it takes a week, a month, or a whole year." But had he really meant a whole year or was that just his way of saying a long time? I took Snow out of his box and we played. I hid some cracker crumbs beneath the mattress and some in another storage room and whistled for him to find them. And he did. Just like he always had. Snow was one smart mouse.

7

I'm Hungry, But
So Are They

I counted the days. I marked them off on the wall with a piece of coal. After a few days, I decided to return to the apartment of the child who read books, where I found some pencils and notebooks that the looters hadn't touched. Maybe I would want to keep a diary. I took a notebook, divided it up into days, and wrote DIARY in big letters on the cover. But that's all I ever wrote except for my name and one sentence on the morning of Day Eight: "I'm getting hungry."

My mind was made up never to go back to the Gryns. I knew that they would have to let me in, since if they didn't I could begin to shout until they were discovered. But first I decided to explore other, more distant houses. Maybe I would find a better hideout in one of them. Maybe I would even find nice people with whom I could stay. But no: No matter what happened, I would have to come back and wait here for father.

Snow was hungry too. I put him in my pocket and cautiously entered the house next door. I had thought it best to go in daytime. At night I'd been hearing more and more footsteps and sounds. Maybe it was just easier to hear at night, or maybe that's when the looters were at work. I worked my way down the street loft by loft until I came to the corner house. Then I climbed downstairs, looked up and down the street, and crossed to the other side. It was the first time that I'd been in any of the houses there. I took Snow from my pocket and whistled for him to find food. It was just an idea that I had. I hadn't hidden anything for him, but maybe he'd be better than me at sniffing something out. And right away he did find some crumbs in a corner. I didn't let him eat them, though, even though the poor mouse squeaked and squeaked. He had to find real food that I could eat too.

At first I was mad at him when he didn't. But then I thought that I wasn't being fair. Maybe there was no food here. I had to be more patient. Only what would happen if father should come in the meantime and not find me? That frightened me so that I snatched Snow up and returned the way I had come.

My first thought was to leave father a note where he could see it. But that would have been pretty dumb. So I wrote a message for him on a brick in a secret code of ours made up of numbers. I hoped that anyone seeing it would think it was just some arithmetic. If it was noticed at all. But even if it seemed suspicious, it was still the only safe way for me to leave "home."

I didn't go out again that day. I stayed hungry. Snow found some old crumbs in Boruch's knapsack. I drank some water and went to sleep.

At the crack of dawn I put Snow in my pocket and we took the same route again. This time I covered it faster, though I still stopped now and then to listen for looters. But I was less afraid than I had been the day before. The one time my heart pounded was when I crossed the street at the corner. How did I know that some looter or informer wasn't watching me from a window? Or that some policeman hadn't set an ambush?

"Snow," I said, "if you don't want to go back to the Gryns — and you know what will happen to you there, don't you? — you've just got to find something to eat."

I walked whistling behind him as though he were a bloodhound. This time I didn't start with the apartments. I decided to look in the lofts first. And then Snow disappeared. I whistled but he didn't come. I crawled along the floor, looking for a hole. For some place he might have squeezed into. I should have taken a flashlight. True, it was daytime, but it was hard to see under the roof. I whistled again and again. How would I manage without my little friend? I felt I was going to cry. Why hadn't I put him on a leash? And then the little sneak turned up again, smacking his lips.

"What have you been eating?"

He didn't say. I looked carefully around me. Yes, there was a hideout here. Part of the loft was missing behind a false wall. It was done so cleverly, though, that you hardly could tell. Was somebody in there? If there was, they would have caught Snow. Except that he might have crept in and out without being seen. Maybe they had heard me and were lying low.

"Open up," I whispered. "I'm a Jewish boy, and I'm looking for food."

There was no answer. But would I have given myself away if I heard someone whisper like that? Of course not. It could be informers using a child as bait, or a woman rat pretending to be a child. I looked around me again. I moved an old chest aside and pushed a board that seemed loose. That was it! Behind it was a small, empty hiding place with half a sack of potatoes. What could I do with them, though? Could you eat raw potatoes? I tasted them. I guessed you certainly could. And then I found a concealed shelf with a bag full of crackers. And some cans of what looked like sardines. And some evaporated milk. And jam. And two jars of chicken fat. And a large bag of flour. And sugar. I ate a handful of it. Then I sat down and had myself a feast. Snow was already asleep in my pocket.

Someone was coming. The people whose hideout it was? I froze in my place. Slowly they came closer. There were two of them. I heard whispers. Maybe even three. The voices were a man's and a woman's. But there were also light footsteps like a child's. The woman said, "I tell you there's someone here!"

"Sit down and don't move, Martha," said the man. "And, you, keep an ear to the stairs in case someone comes."

I'd made a bad mistake by not replacing the board and the chest.

"Aha!" said the man when he saw me eating. He fell on the food himself. "Come!" he called to his wife and daughter.

They came. The girl had a polka dot dress on. They sat down and stuffed themselves with my food as though I weren't even there.

"Who else is hiding here?" asked the man with a mouth full of food.

So that's why they were eating so fast. But that only

dawned on me afterward, when it was already too late. And only then did I realize what I should have answered. I should have said: "My father and my uncles, and if you're not out of here before they're back they'll . . ." Or something like that. But instead I blurted out without thinking, "This isn't my hideout. But I found the food."

"So did I," said the man.

He stopped eating and began to dump it into a sack that his wife was holding.

"It's my food!" I shouted.

"If you don't shut up, you little fool," he said, "I'll beat the daylights out of you." He slapped me in the face.

"Leave him alone, Marek," said his wife. "And, you," she said to me, "don't you dare shout."

The girl must have been eight or nine. I couldn't tell exactly. She looked at me curiously and ate some sugar. She seemed nice.

They finished filling the sack and turned to go.

"I found the food," I said again. "You can't take it all."

"Where are you hiding?" asked the man. "How many of you are there?"

"There's just me," I said.

I shouldn't have told them the truth now either. I should have said that there were a lot of us, and that we were strong enough to find their hideout and teach them a lesson they wouldn't forget.

"Where?" asked the man.

I shrugged.

"Give him some food," said the woman all of a sudden.

"The hell I will," said the man. "He'll be caught soon anyway. And we can hold out till the end of the war if only we find enough to eat."

He handed the full sack to his wife and picked up the half-sack of potatoes. They started to go. I followed them.

The man waved his fist at me. "Scram!"

I didn't say anything. I kept walking behind them without getting too close. The man put down his sack and made a lunge for me. I dodged and ran to the far end of the loft. He ran after me. His wife and daughter ran after him.

"I didn't know there was a passage here," he said. "The boy must have come from the next house."

"What will you do if you catch him?"

"I'll throttle him," he said angrily.

"Don't be ridiculous," said the woman. "Suppose that it was Martha, and that she was all on her own."

Are women always nicer than men? Maybe. Except of course for the Amazons. I once read about them in a book.

They picked up the sacks again. I followed them once more, keeping an eye on their movements.

"Papa," said the girl. "Give him some food."

"Shut your mouth, Martha," he said. But he stopped and put down his sack.

He sighed. Then he took the other sack from his wife and pulled out some crackers, a can of evaporated milk, and a jar of jam. His wife picked up an old newspaper from the floor and made a little bag for sugar just like grocers did.

"That's enough," the man scolded.

They put it all down on the floor and told me to take it. I didn't budge. So they picked up their sacks and went. I took what they left me and started back. It wasn't much. Barely enough for three days. Or maybe four, since I had already eaten today. But every day counted. Every day father might come.

 **8**

The Pistol Really Shoots

I had planned to go out again the next day, even though I was afraid to push my luck. Still, there was always a chance I'd find food left behind in some apartment. At least I hoped so. I was on my way out when I heard shots and the sound of a car. It was definitely coming from the ghetto and not from the Polish side. I decided to stay in the cellar. I sat near the opening and tried hard to listen. I heard shouts far away; then silence. It went on like that all morning.

A house-to-house search. My turn came in the afternoon. I waited to see them enter the building and then retreated deeper into the cellar. It was clear to me now why Boruch had always said that a hideout without a second exit wasn't worth a damn.

There were German soldiers and Polish policemen. I thought I saw a Jewish policeman too. The soldiers had some kind of strange instruments. After a while I heard them knocking and tapping. They must have been looking for bunkers. They came to the entrance to the cellar and stopped to examine it. One of them said in German, "We should widen this hole and look inside."

"No one could possibly get through there," said someone else.

I heard scraping noises and laughter. I peeked out of my storage room and saw someone trying to squeeze inside. It must have made the others laugh, because he could hardly get his booted foot through the hole. Then I heard them searching outside the building, and finally they left.

I stayed where I was until evening. But I knew now that my hideout wasn't good enough. And then, for the first time, I began to think of the broken third floor that hung out over the ruins at the back of the building. It would have been perfect if only I knew how to fly.

The best thing about it was that it was protected on all sides. No one could see onto it, neither from inside the house nor from any of the other houses on the street. Unless, that is, I were to look out the window, in which case I could be seen from the Polish side. If there was really a larder up there, like the one whose remains we had found on the second floor, I could keep Snow and my things in it. And if I could manage to get up to the fourth floor, I'd have myself a duplex apartment. Only what would I do for an emergency exit? I couldn't jump to the street from that high up. But I could lower myself by a rope.

I started to think about ropes. Why, I was an expert on them! That's when I had the idea of a rope ladder. I could pull it up after me and no one would know I was there. How could anyone be on the floor of a ruins that couldn't be reached? The one problem was getting up the first time to make the rope ladder fast.

I would have to build a wooden ladder first. A very high one. I doubted that I could find boards long enough for it, but I could nail shorter ones together. It would only have to hold me once. But I would have to build it outside the cellar, since it wouldn't fit through the opening, and that wasn't so simple. The hammering would be heard. Someone would come to investigate. At night it might even be heard on the Polish side, maybe during the day too. No, it was a rotten plan . . .

I knew lots of fairy tales about animals and people. Usually the person was a prince or poor farmer lad who had once done a favor to a bee or a fish and was then in return helped by it to get out of some fix. Like to find the keys to a castle that had fallen to the bottom of the sea. But no matter how hard I stared at the birds that flapped above the fourth floor, I couldn't think of any favor I might do them. And even if I thought of one, what could they do for me?

I ate and lay down to sleep. I must have tossed and turned a long time before I dozed off. In the middle of the night — no, it was already toward morning — I dreamed that I was angry at the birds for waking me so early every day. And in my dream I picked up a rock and threw it at them. Over and over again. One rock flew through the window and landed on the Polish side, where it hit the bully who used to stone us before the transports began. He started to scream like a frightened woman and I awoke. Someone really was screaming. It was a woman in the street. Not on the Polish side, though. On ours. She was screaming not far from me, although the sound kept fading more and more.

Now I knew how to get the rope ladder up to the third floor. It would be a cinch. Sometimes, when I had trouble solving some riddle or problem in arithmetic, father used to say, "Why don't you sleep on it, son."

And only if I did, and still didn't know the answer in the morning, would he agree to help me.

I had my plan. I would go to the rope factory, even though it was three long blocks away. If I wanted to make an honest hideout, I had to take the risk. I would bring rope, find tools in some apartment, and saw wood for the ladder rungs. Short boards could be found, and I'd saw them deep in the cellar: If I could hear nothing from there, no one would hear me either. Just to be on the safe side, though, I'd work by day when the noise from the Polish street drowned other sounds out.

Besides heavy rope for the ladder, I'd need a long piece of thin rope too. I'd tie one end of it to a rock and throw it through the third-floor window. I might not succeed at first, but sooner or later I was sure to. Not during the day. I'd do it at night, when no one on the Polish side would notice a rock flying suddenly through an empty window and descending slowly along the wall of a house with a long rope dragging behind it.

The rock would pull the rope after it. I'd wait for it to drop past the second-floor window, from which I'd reach out and grab it. Then I'd tie the rope ladder to the rope's other end and haul in the rock until the ladder was hoisted to the third floor. After that I'd make the rock-end fast and climb up.

Suppose, though, that there was a guard in the rope factory? I'd just have to chance it. I explained that to Snow while I fed him some cracker crumbs spread with chicken fat from the jar. I petted his white fur gently and told him my plan. Then I put him back in his box, took the pistol, and slipped into the house next door. The first thing I did was go through all the apartments again in search of tools. Almost at once I found a case with a red cross on its lid, but it only had bandages and medicines. In the end I found a small workroom with what I was looking for. I took a saw and a few other tools that perhaps I would need some day, left them in a hidden corner of the staircase, and continued on my way.

By now I felt sure of myself as far as the corner house, and I moved quickly and even carelessly, not stopping even once to listen, until I reached the loft where I had found and lost the food. Even before I heard the scream I had a feeling that something was wrong. Perhaps I'd heard noises without being aware of them.

"Papa!" shouted a small girl.

It wasn't an ordinary shout for someone to come. It was a scream for help. I stood perfectly still. My first reaction was to run. But then I thought that maybe it was Martha. I headed for the scream. Suddenly I heard a man laugh brutally. I stepped up to the passage that led to the next loft. In the dim light beyond the wall I saw a large man with a big sack on his back dragging a girl by the arm. I strained to get a glimpse of her. I couldn't make out her face, but I recognized the polka dot dress. Without thinking, I drew the pistol, cocked it, and released the safety catch. The man heard the click and spun around.

"Leave her alone!" I said in the deepest voice I could make.

And I fired.

The shot scared the pants off me. The bullet hit a wall and I heard plaster fly in all directions. There was a strange smell too. It must have been the gunpowder that father had told me about. For the first time since I'd set eyes on the gun, I realized that it really could shoot. I guess I'd never quite believed it until then.

It certainly had an effect. The big oaf let go of the girl, threw down his sack, and ran for dear life. If I hadn't been so frightened by the shot, I would have burst out laughing. Martha was too scared to move. I was sure she would have run away too if she could have.

I slipped through the passageway.

"It's just me," I said. "The boy whose food you took, remember?"

I took a step toward her. She backed away as though I were a German.

"You ate some sugar and your father tried to grab me, remember? I know your name's Martha."

She stood still.

"Who was that who shouted?"

I couldn't manage to make my voice as deep as before. Still, it came out pretty low.

"It was me." I thought I saw her smile.

"And what was that big bang?"

"It was just a rock I knocked against some tin," I explained.

"It was like . . . a real shot," she said shakily. "It even chipped stuff off the wall." She pointed behind her.

I said nothing.

"What will happen if he comes back?" she said in a worried voice.

"Where did you come from?"

"From our hideout. I'm not supposed to leave it. But my parents went to look for more food and I thought I'd just come out for some air. It's so dark and stuffy in there. And then all of a sudden he came."

"Come," I suggested. "Let's wait for your parents in your hideout."

She didn't answer. Then she stepped close to me and whispered, "I'm not allowed to tell where it is. My father would kill me."

"All right," I said. "Let's go to the loft next door and hide there in a corner."

"What if my parents come back and don't find me?"

I was dying to talk with someone, even if it was only a girl. But I couldn't force her to stay, as much as I tried dragging it out.

"How old are you?"

"Nine."

"I thought you were only eight."

"That's because I'm small. How old are you?"

"Twelve. Actually, eleven and a half. Where did you live before?"

"In the ghetto." She told me where they had lived before the transports, and where they had lived before the war. Then she told me about the dolls she used to have. She had only one of them left, plus another her father had found in an apartment. I told her about my mouse. That scared her.

"You really touch it?"

"Yes."

"And it doesn't bite or give you germs?"

That made me laugh. I'd forgotten how scared some people were of mice. Like old Boruch. "You know, human beings have been raising mice for three thousand years."

"How do you know?"

"It's in the encyclopedia."

"I'd better get back to our hideout," she said all at once.

I nodded.

"Where will you go from here?"

"All the way to the rope factory. I have to get something there."

"Aren't you afraid?"

"Sometimes."

Before she left, she took a pin from her hair and gave it to me. I listened to her going down the stairs and then went to look at my present in the light. I hadn't even told her my name.

Looters

A portable iron ladder led down from the loft of the factory. I checked to see if it was stable, the way father always did, clambered down it, and tiptoed through the building. Everything was under lock and key, the door to the storeroom too. I looked out into the yard. There was a watchman there. He wore a leather coat and boots, and sat smoking on a bench beneath a poplar tree. I had never seen him in the factory before. If only he wasn't there, and if only there was an empty window, I could enter the storeroom from the yard. If. . . . Reluctantly I decided to head back, collect all the laundry lines I could find in the lofts, and splice a thick rope out of them. But I made no move to go.

It had been a second home for us, the factory. Of course, it was run by the Germans, but Boruch and father had worked in it since the winter. The watchman glanced up at my window as though he felt my eyes on him. I stood slightly away from it without moving. He didn't see me. He sat a while longer, then rose and paced up and down in the yard. Suddenly there was a knock on the front gate. Not just a knock. Two of them. And then a pause. And three more knocks. And another pause. And five knocks in a row. And still another pause. And one last knock. The watchman went to the gate, which creaked as he opened it. I knew that sound well.

Two nervous-looking men stepped into the yard.

"Did anyone see you?" asked the watchman angrily. "I thought I told you to come after dark!"

They tried making excuses. I couldn't hear exactly what they said, because they spoke in hushed tones and had their backs to me. The watchman entered the building and I retreated back up to the safety of the top floor. Then I heard the storeroom door open. Bales of rope were tossed out a window into the yard. Thieves, I thought. Some large sacks followed. The three men emerged, stuffed the rope into the sacks, and tied each sack. It was just the right rope for me, both the heavy and the thin kind.

They dragged the tied sacks to the gate, where I lost sight of them. I heard the gate open and bang shut again, and then the three of them walk away up the street. There was silence. I hurried to the gate and tried lifting a sack. It was too heavy for me. I lifted another, lighter one, cut its knot with my penknife, looked to see what was in it, retied it, and dragged it up the stairs. It wasn't easy to get it up the ladder, which I pulled after me too, because it was exactly what I would need to climb from the third to the fourth floor of the ruin. I carried first the sack, then the ladder, to the passage leading out to the roof. I had to leave the ladder. I couldn't drag it over the roof in broad daylight. There was simply no way of moving with it quickly while crouched on the planks used by the chimney sweeps to get around up there. I would have to come back for it at night.

On my way back up Bird Street with the sack I stopped off at our old house. There wasn't any reason not to. Already on the way to the factory I had been tempted to look in on it. Maybe even to go down to the bunker and ask the Gryns for more food.

The apartment was a wreck. Everything of value had been taken. The furniture was thrown all around. I couldn't bear the sight of it, so like all the other apartments that I'd been in. Well, why should it have been any different? I went to the bathroom to signal the Gryns. Just thinking of them made me mad.

In the ghetto, in the days before the transports, I used to hold my breath whenever I passed someone I didn't like in the street. It didn't have to be anyone I knew. It was just something I felt I had to do. Not because whoever it was didn't smell good, but because I didn't want his "air" in my lungs. I would imagine that "air" like the wake of a boat, and I wouldn't breathe again till I was past it. The first time I met the Gryns I took a deep breath and held it. Later, of course, when they started dropping by our room, I couldn't do that anymore. And then when we built the bunker with them, I had to breathe their "air" all the time. But I never did get to like them.

There was a large hole in the floor where the toilet had been ripped out. My heart sank. Already I regretted thinking mean things about the Gryns. Poor Yossi. The wooden ladder that father and I had made of sawed chair legs was still in place. I climbed down it. It was dark below and there was a funny smell. I saw no sign of life. Perhaps the same day that the Germans had tried to enter my cellar they had searched for bunkers all along the street. Or else someone had ratted. I didn't want to think about it. And yet I couldn't help remembering the shots I had heard. And the woman's screams. Although it could have been another woman too.

The candles and matches were still where we had put them. I lit a candle and went to look at the cupboard. It was bare. I went to the emergency food cache. It too was broken into and gone. Someone had known where the bunker was and where we kept our food. Had father been here? Impossible. And then I remembered the man who had helped us to build the opening beneath the toilet, a former construction worker. Only he had been transported long ago. Or had he been? Perhaps he too was a rat.

I ran back to the ladder. The sooner I got out of here, the better. Suddenly I tripped. The candle fell and went out. I felt around me. My hand touched something soft. I groped my way to the candles; this time I decided to take them and the matches with me. I had stumbled on a small shoulder bag that belonged to one of the children. Perhaps to Yossi. I took it and hurried up the stairs, not stopping to rest until I'd reached the loft. There I sat down on my sack to catch my breath.

In the bag were some bottles of water and the usual things: four cans of evaporated milk, some crackers, some sugar cubes, a jar of fat, some chocolate. There was also the little teddy bear that Yossi always slept with. The straps of the bag were missing. I attached a piece of rope to it and moved on.

At first I tried dragging the two things together through the passageways between lofts. But soon I was exhausted and had to take them one at a time: first Yossi's bag and then the sack of rope. Sometimes, just for a change, I did it the other way around.

It was getting dark out. That morning it had drizzled, but it wasn't raining now. I came to the corner house of the second street between the factory and my ruin. I had the sack of rope with me; the bag was already downstairs, hidden behind the front gate. All at once someone leaped through a passage from the next building without noticing me in the dark hallway. Someone else ran after him and caught him. They began to argue, at first in whispers, then at the tops of their voices. In slow motion I slipped into an apartment to hide. I almost screamed. In the weak light coming from the window I saw a third man standing with some suits draped over his arm. He put a finger to his lips and whispered to me to be quiet. I didn't let out a peep.

We listened to the quarrel in the hallway. Apparently it was over a box of jewelry. Soon it went from words and shouts to blows. One of the men yelled, "Don't, you bastard! Put that knife down!" And then: "Jesus!" And a thud. Then a single set of running footsteps could be heard until they were gone.

The man with the suits told me not to move. I could tell from how he talked to me that he took me for a looter like himself.

"I'd better go see if he's still alive," he said, and went out to the hallway to look.

I waited a second to make sure that he was gone and took off like a shot. Except that I chose the wrong direction. In my eagerness to escape, I ran right into him.

"Were you trying to give me the slip?" he asked.

"Yes," I said. He wasn't at all frightening.

"Well, let's get out of here," he said, wiping his bloody fingers on the curtain.

I followed him down to the courtyard, where he sat in an abandoned armchair and laid the suits across his knees. I stood and smiled at him. I remembered mother's advice: "Trust people and appeal to the good in their hearts, and they'll never do you any harm." And yet father had said: ". . . Trust only yourself."

"So what's in that sack, young fellow?"

"Rope."

"From the factory?"

"Yes."

"What do you intend to do with it?"

"It's for my father."

"Tell your father that next time he should come by himself and not send a child to risk his neck for him."

"If I told him that he'd hit me," I said.

He sighed. I didn't mind his "air" at all.

"All right, then," he said. "How are you getting out of the ghetto?"

"My father will wait for me at the wall with a ladder," I said. "And how about you?"

He paused to consider. "I know a secret way out of here. I'd even tell you about it, except that I can't trust you any more than you can trust me. But that's war for you. My secret mustn't ever become known to the Germans. A pity, eh?"

It certainly was. I shrugged. Then I asked if he wanted to hear a joke.

He smiled and said, "Sure, as long as it's a clean one."

We both laughed. I told him the joke about the two men who argued what time it was. One of them said: It's morn-

ing. The other said: No, it's evening. I'm telling you that
it's morning! said the first. Can't you see that it's evening?!
said the second, getting angry. They kept it up until a third
man happened by. They stopped him and said: Please ex-
cuse us, but is it morning or evening? The man thought it
over for a while and then he said: I'm sorry, but I'm from
out of town.

We both laughed again.

That was one of father's lessons: "With the Poles you've
got to sound confident, even a little bit cheeky. And you've
got to make them laugh."

I wasn't sure how you made someone laugh, and so I told
the joke. It worked.

"I can't tell you my secret route, young fellow," said the
man. "But if you ever need help, come see me and I'll see
what I can do." He gave me his address. It was a street I
knew. Before the war we used to pass it on the way to my
grandmother's house. It wasn't far from Bird Street, in fact.
That is, it wouldn't have been if there hadn't been a wall
between them.

"Ask for Bolek," he said. "I'm the doorman there.
What's your name?"

"Alex."

He rose and stepped up to me. I didn't move away. He
felt the sack on my back and said:

"It's rope, all right."

We parted. He went back into the house and I ran across
the street with the rope. Then I came back for Yossi's bag.
It was strange that a nice man like that had come to steal
clothes. He looked like he might have been a teacher before
the war. What wouldn't people do for money? Yet mother
always said there are things that money can't buy.

10

The Larder and
the Bird Floor

Early the next morning, as soon as life began on the Polish side of the wall, I found some boards near my ruin and carried them deep into the cellar to saw rungs for a ladder. Usually, when I sawed wood with father, my job was holding the wood. Or else, if we used the big two-handled saw, I pulled it the easy way and he pulled it back the hard way. But this time I had a small handsaw. I put one foot on a board and started to saw. At first I sawed too quickly and tired myself out, but soon I found the right pace. The work went at a good clip.

It wasn't hard to make the rope ladder, because I had learned to tie all kinds of knots in the factory. My one problem was not knowing exactly how high it should be. I found a pole and tried measuring the distance. Not all at once. First from the ground floor to the second floor. Then to the second-floor window. Then (standing against the wall, of course, so no one on the Polish side could see) the height of the window itself. Finally I guessed the distance from the top of the window to the floor above it, and doubled it to be on the safe side. As far as I could tell, all of the floors were about the same height. I could have done a better job with a yardstick, but I managed pretty well as it was.

The fact was, though, that I had been getting a bit careless about moving around inside the building as though there were no danger of being surprised from the street. I had better be more cautious. It was awful to think that if I was caught father might come and not find me and decide that I was dead.

I had sawed more wood than I needed, and when the ladder was finished I threw the extra pieces into one of the storage rooms. Then I sat down to chat with Snow until it got dark. This time Snow and I didn't talk about what we would do after the war. Neither did I tell him the same old jokes that weren't even funny anymore. Instead I explained to him just how I meant to hoist the ladder up to the third floor. It was just too bad that I had to do it in the dark, because I was a pretty good shot with a stone when I could see. And the window was a big target. My only fear was that I wouldn't have enough light. There were blackouts on the Polish side just like on ours, because of the war with the Russians. When did the moon come up?

As soon as it grew dark I started to carry out my plan. It worked perfectly. I tied a rock to the end of a rope and threw. The first two times I missed and hit the bottom floor above me. (I mean, of course, the third floor, but from now on I'll call it the bottom floor, and the fourth floor the top floor, because it's simpler.) Well, I hadn't promised Snow that I'd pitch that rock through the window on my first try. And on my third it flew right through. After that it was easy.

The rock dragged the rope down after it along the wall

of the building until I saw it against the sky from the second-floor window and grabbed hold of it. Then I tied the ladder to the rope's other end and pulled on the rock. As soon as the top rung reached the bottom floor, I made the rock end of the rope fast to a beam sticking out of the ruins. It still wasn't a finished ladder, because being held by only one rope caused it to twist when I climbed so that the rungs were as though ironed flat. Still, even edge-down they gave me enough footing to get to the bottom floor.

And what a perfect hideout it would make! Of course, it was awfully dirty. I started to kick the rubble off of it and stopped: I mustn't make such loud sounds at night. Then I found a piece of pipe sticking out of the wall and tied the top of the ladder to it, struggling to see in the darkness with my flashlight, which I was afraid to use for more than a few seconds at a time even though I shielded it with one hand. Now the ladder hung the way it should. It swung but stayed straight, like the ladder of a ship. I climbed up and down again. It took me a while to get the hang of it. After all, it still wasn't the same as a ladder made of metal or wood. Within a few days, though, I was scrambling up and down it like a monkey.

It turned out to be a lucky thing that I'd made the ladder an extra length, because I hadn't taken into account that the ruins beneath the bottom floor were lower than where I had measured from. In fact, the ladder rose a good floor-and-a-half from them. There were thirteen rungs on it, a lucky number. Not for everyone perhaps, but certainly for me.

Boruch, for instance, once told me that all the bad things in his life had happened either on the thirteenth day of the month, the thirteenth month of the year, or the thirteenth hour of the day. "But there is no thirteen o'clock," I protested. Yes, there was, he said: It was the same as one P.M. It didn't even occur to me to tell him that the year had only twelve months.

"Of course, it's just a superstition," said mother. "But if you believe in those things, your beliefs can influence what happens."

"Did you ever notice, dear," said father, "that our street has no Number Thirteen?"

She hadn't. The numbers on our side of the street, father said, went straight from eleven to fifteen. No landlord wanted to own Number 13 because no tenant would want to live in it.

I couldn't resist running out to the street to see if he was right.

The larder on the bottom floor was in the same place beneath the window as the remains of the larder below. It still had its doors, though. And how roomy it was! I lit a candle inside it to see if the light showed through any cracks. It did in only one place. I covered it and tried again. Now there was nothing. I would be able to read at night without being discovered and without even breaking the blackout.

There were some shelves on the wall too. It was like a real house, with places to put things and corners to sleep in and doors to open and shut. And as for an emergency exit, nothing was simpler. I'd bring up some rope and tie it to the pipe. If I had to clear out in a hurry, I'd throw it out the window and slide down. But that could wait until the morning.

I returned to the cellar and told Snow. "Tomorrow is moving day!"

Mother had laughed when she said that the night before we moved to the ghetto. Yet I saw the tears glint in her eyes. She had tried explaining to me how nice our new apartment would be, because it was so small that we would all be together in one room, with only a curtain between us. Hadn't I always wanted to sleep in the same room with them?

She was right. I always had.

"As long as we're alive and well," said father.

I told Snow that the ladder was hanging in place, and that . . . but I never finished my sentence. Yes, it was hanging there in the dark, where someone entering the building and poking about the ruins might not notice it, but what would happen in the morning? Suppose there was another house-to-house search? I couldn't just leave it there. How could it be gotten up to the bottom floor, though, before I went to sleep in the cellar? By climbing up, pulling it after me, and sliding back down on a rope? But then how would I get it down again in the morning? It was too much for me to think about in one day. I took my blanket, my pillow, and a sheet to spread on the rubble. And of course, Snow and his box. I tied them with a rope and struggled up the ladder with the bundle around my waist. Then I thought some more, climbed down again, and packed what food I had left. Triumphantly, I climbed back up with it, pulled the ladder after me, crawled into the larder, and shut the doors behind me for the night. For the moment my worries were over.

There were two air vents in the larder, round holes in the wall of the building with metal slats that could be opened or closed. Just like in our house before the ghetto. I fell asleep with a wonderful feeling of having struck it rich.

Early the next morning, as soon as I heard the cars and wagons on the Polish side, I cleaned the floor and brushed all the dirt down below. Then I quickly brought up the rest of my things: my clothes, the water bottles, and my books. The mattress was too heavy. In its place I would fetch a few quilts from the house next door. And then it occurred to me to try the faucet in the sink. If there was water on the top floor, why not here?

I counted to three and turned it hard. There was water. Just like on the bird floor above. I had carried all those full bottles up for nothing. And they weighed a lot too. I should have realized that there would be water here. How did the old proverb go? If you don't use your head, you'll have to use your legs. Well, I had used mine until they hurt.

When everything was brought up, I remembered that I still had a problem. How could I go anywhere without leaving the ladder hanging down? I decided to try an experiment. I tied a rope to the bottom rung and ran it through the metal ring on the third-floor window that once had turned to lock the window frame in place. Then I threw the rope down, climbed after it, and pulled on it from below. The ladder folded and started to rise but stopped halfway to the floor. Yet even if it had risen all the way, the rope would still have been seen.

I solved the second problem first. The house had been built long ago, and the electric wires, which were attached to the walls at a later date, now dangled everywhere, torn and at loose ends. I untied the rope and substituted a long wire. No one who saw it hanging down from the bottom floor would suspect a thing. I was sure of that.

I experimented some more with the ladder. Eventually I

hit on a solution for it too. I ran the wire over a metal rod that stuck out from the top floor, that is, from the ceiling above me. Now I could hoist the ladder almost up to the rod and then let it fall on the floor by the larder. As for retrieving it from below, I simply tied another wire to the bottom rung and let it hang straight down. One pull and the ladder was on the ground.

I was pretty bushed when I was finished, partly from climbing up and down with all those heavy things, partly from being so tense that I kept twisting my neck to look at the front gate, and partly from straining my mind with so many thoughts. Father would have laughed to hear me say that, but mother always claimed that strenuous mental work was as fatiguing as any other kind. I guess she knew, because she did a lot of it herself.

That afternoon I slipped into the house next door and brought back two quilts and some blankets for the floor and the walls of the larder. When night came, I shut the doors behind me and fed Snow. Then I let him run around loose. There was no way for him to escape. Lying there with my eyes closed, I heard noises from the Polish side. Before, down in the cellar, they barely had reached me. Now, though, I could actually hear human voices. They sounded far away, because I was high above them, but now and then I made out what they said.

I blew out the candle and opened an air vent. The moon rose and I could see the whole street, even the storefronts that the wall had always hid. It was dark and deserted because of the blackout and the curfew. All of a sudden someone approached a house. A door opened and a large patch of light was cast onto the sidewalk and the street. Inside I saw a large room full of smoke and people sitting at small tables. Now I realized that the music I sometimes heard at night did not come from a radio, as I had thought, but from this place, which must have been some kind of tavern. The door shut and it was dark again. It was deathly quiet outside. But in each of those houses lived Poles.

I told Snow that in the morning I would go get the metal ladder from the factory. I wanted a home with two larders and a terrace full of birds.

11

The Bunker

I had decided to rise very early, when the light was still gray. That way, I thought, the daytime looters would still be in bed and the nighttime ones would already have gone home. But despite the chirping of the birds on the floor above me, I didn't wake up in time. When I stepped out of the larder it was already a fine autumn day. I stretched and stifled a yawn. I tried to glimpse the front gate but couldn't see it. Which meant that anyone entering the building couldn't see me either. I moved forward and it came into sight. Now I could see the ruins beneath me too. I knelt with a red crayon that I had taken from the children's room next door and drew a line on the floor that mustn't be passed standing up. Then I drew a second line in green that mustn't be passed on my knees.

I sat in the doorway of the larder and had breakfast with Snow. All of a sudden I heard a car coming up the street, on the ghetto side of the wall. I put everything back in the larder and shut the door, even though I knew that it couldn't be seen from the ground. I remained where I was, stretched out on the floor.

They came straight to Number 78. Would they have sent a car just for me? Maybe I'd been so active the last few days that I'd been heard and mistaken for many people. And yet I had tried to be as quiet as I could. Could someone have seen me putting up the ladder and only now come to check on me? I'd throw the emergency rope out the window and make a run for it. I readied myself. Except that Snow was inside the larder. I should never have left him there, because taking him out would make noise.

A large group of men entered the ruins. I could tell there were a lot of them by their footsteps and shouts, which were partly in German and partly in Yiddish. Someone said something in good Polish and was answered in bad. I heard things being dragged over the ruins, and then an order given in German and bricks being struck and falling down. Plaster crumbled and showered to the ground. I realized what they were doing and relaxed. They had already spoken of it the first time they came here looking for a bunker. Now they were widening the opening in order to search the cellar.

I tried to imagine myself down there. What would it be like to be sitting there now, cringing helplessly and listening to the strokes of the hammers and picks?

The birds on the floor above me took to the air and flew off.

It didn't take them long to break through the opening. Then I heard more banging. And muffled shouts from deep within the cellar. They weren't looking for me. They were looking for bigger game. Could it be that under the floor of the cellar in which I had lived for twelve days was a bunker with people in it? And that I hadn't heard them make a sound while all along they heard me? But maybe they hadn't heard me either.

Father and Boruch had spoken of bunkers like that. Not makeshift ones like ours. Real ones, dug deep underground, with running water and concealed tunnels for air. Even with bathrooms and septic tanks. (Father explained to me what a septic tank was — a kind of sewage system without pipes.) Bunkers stockpiled with enough food to last for a long, long time. The trouble was that too many people were involved in building such a place, even if they were all supposed to hide in it afterward. Except for the man who would seal it in the end by flooring over the entrance.

There was a sharp explosion. Plaster fell on me from above. For a panicky moment I thought the whole top floor would collapse on me. Then there was silence. And then a sound of screaming and wailing that seemed to come from deep in the earth. Followed by shots, which sounded near. I prayed that they were just warning shots fired outside the bunker.

Its inhabitants began to come out. No one was screaming anymore. The children just cried and some of the grown-ups groaned and sighed. I didn't dare move forward on the floor to get a look at them. Someone might glance up and see me.

It took a long while for the last of them to emerge. The Germans and the policemen kept shouting, and footsteps kept crossing the ruins from the cellar to the front gate. Now and then someone stumbled. Plaster and bricks tumbled down. Somebody fell once or maybe twice. A shot rang out. Nobody screamed, though. Even the children had stopped crying. The last footsteps left the building. I heard voices in the street and an order to line up in threes. The same as had been given us. Then they were marched away. A few more shots. Finally the car started up and drove off.

The sun shone straight down on the ruins. It was noon. I crept quietly into the larder and didn't come out again until evening. It was strange to think that all those people had been hiding with me in one house without us even knowing about each other.

I took a flashlight and the pistol. They'd never take me away like that. That was for sure. I lowered the ladder and climbed down. All kinds of junk was scattered on the ground between the cellar and the gate. I entered the cellar through the big opening that had been made. About half-way down the corridor there was a large hole in the ground. I shone the light through it and saw a low, long room that looked like a bomb shelter. Could that really have been what it was? But no, that didn't make sense: The tenants of the building had had the cellar for air raids. Wooden steps led down from the hole. How had the Germans known where they were? They had gone straight to the secret entrance.

I climbed down. The place was a shambles. Wooden benches with mattresses lined the walls. Tables stood in the middle of the room. On one of them were scattered some cards. On another lay an upside-down chessboard. On a third, large metal one stood some pots, pans, and kerosene burners. I went over to it and began to eat without thinking. Boiled potatoes. Rice. Cooked carrots. I hadn't eaten vegetables for ages. In one of the pans was an omelet. It wasn't so good, though. I knew the taste: It came from salt eggs. And there was a whole pantry full of food.

I was sure they'd come back for it, and so I set to work. I

couldn't carry whole sackfuls of things, so I poured them out on the ground and took what I could. Two trips for potatoes. Two trips for crackers. One trip for rice, although I doubted it would be safe to cook it. But I decided to take a pot, pan, and kerosene burner anyway. And a jerrycan of kerosene. It was awfully heavy. I looked around and found another that was only half full. I carried it up, came down again, half emptied another can, and took that up too. My larder was bursting. There was hardly room in it for me anymore. If only I had a way of getting up to the top floor! It was a shame that I couldn't make another rope ladder. That is, I could make one all right, because I had lots of rope and wood, but there was no fifth-floor ceiling to attach a wire to in order to pull the ladder back up from below. I thought again of the metal ladder in the factory. Risking going back for it was the last thing I wanted to do. Lately there were too many people poking around the empty houses on the way. No one could guarantee that the next looter I ran into would be as nice as Bolek. I had even memorized his address. Just to be sure, I said it over to myself every night like a child reciting its prayers.

I went down again and carried up a big iron pot of salt eggs. They were better than nothing. There was a sack of carrots there too. Some of them were rotten. I picked out the good ones. Carrots could be eaten raw. And they helped you to see in the dark. I knew that from mother.

And then I went to the bathroom, and even flushed. Like a king! When I was done, I took a look around me and threw some odds and ends over the potatoes that I had dumped on the ground and over the rice and kerosene. It looked more natural that way. As though looters had been here. Then I gave in to temptation, found a towel and soap, undressed, and took a shower. Incredibly, the water was hot. I let it run on and on until it began to cool. The bunker had a tin boiler with an oil heater beneath it, just like the one we had at home. If the Germans didn't wreck the place, I could come back to wash now and then. Not too often, though. I didn't want to push my luck.

At home I really had hated to wash. Before each bath I'd have a big fight with mother. Now, though, it was delicious.

After I was dressed again, I put some jars of jam and chicken fat in a sack and carried it up tied to my waist. I worked in total darkness. By now I knew each step by heart. I found a few boxes of sugar cubes and some chocolate. And a small binoculars and some children's books. The one thing I didn't see was sardines. I'd expected to find some because I'd seen some opened cans of them in the garbage. Perhaps the policemen had taken them.

That brought me back to earth with a start. They were certain to return.

Early the next morning they did, and took everything. I could hear them cursing and swearing. In the afternoon two German soldiers arrived. I couldn't see them, but I heard their voices. They spent some time in the building, exchanged a few words, and suddenly ran outside. There was a moment of silence and then a terrific boom. Everything shook and part of the top floor crashed down on my floor. Poor Snow trembled in my hand. He must have thought it was the end of the world. Long afterward loose bricks and beams still kept falling. I waited for night to come before I climbed down to see what had happened. They had dynamited the entrance to the cellar. It couldn't be gotten into anymore.

12

The Girl Who Did Homework

I didn't go get the ladder from the factory, because it occurred to me that there must be one like it nearer by in one of the lofts, which I had never bothered to inspect very carefully on my trips through them. And sure enough, I found just what I was looking for, except that it couldn't be moved. I had to bring tools and unscrew it. That was scary, because I kept hearing voices and footsteps from the next house. In the end, though, I finished before dark and brought the ladder back to my new home.

It was the autumn before the revolt in Ghetto A, and I had been living alone now for two months. I had everything worked out to perfection. Up above, on the top floor, I kept my stores. The larder on the bottom floor was my bedroom and kitchen. By kitchen I mean that I cooked in it on the burner. I'd shut the air vents and make potatoes or even rice. I wasn't sure how to cook rice, so I just put it in water and boiled it until it was soft. Then I'd eat the sticky mush with jam. It wasn't like mother's rice, in which every grain was separate, but so what?

As long as the eggs lasted I made myself omelets, too. I

didn't cook the carrots. I ate them quickly before they started to rot.

All during those months the Germans kept returning with Polish moving men to strip the houses all around. I could hear trucks come and go, and workers shouting. Sometimes something heavy would fly through a window and smash to pieces on the sidewalk below. There was always wild laughter when that happened. It must have been some big piece of furniture that couldn't be gotten down the stairs or wasn't worth the effort. Once I peeked out the front gate and saw a huge grand piano being lowered by ropes from the house across the street.

By day, the Germans made their rounds with their moving men and police, and by night, the looters came. Whenever I got so bored that I felt I had to get out, I'd wait for early morning or early evening. Those were the safest times. There were police patrols then, too, but they never entered any buildings. They just kept an eye on the streets. The looters had their own ways of getting in and out of the ghetto.

The first few times I left the ruin I was afraid that father might come, not find me there, and go away. I didn't trust the marked brick, even though I had written in code on several other bricks, too. In the end I hit on another way of leaving a message. I took some chalky white plaster and on the walls I drew arrows leading in from the street as though they were part of some children's game. I even faced one the wrong way as a decoy, and marked the "treasure" with an arrow pointing down. Beneath it I put a brick over an old, yellowed scrap of paper on which I had written: "You're very warm. Don't give up. Alex."

It was really too bad that I couldn't use the bathroom and the shower that were buried in the bunker, because I was afraid to go farther down the street. Once a day, in the morning or evening, I'd slip into the building next door, but since I didn't dare make noise by flushing the toilet so near my hideout, I simply went to the bathroom in the general mess and hid it there to keep looters and informers from guessing that someone lived nearby. That was my daily adventure. There was no choice. As for peeing, I used the sink. Once I tried to see where the drainpipe ran but lost it among the ruins. Well, it had to be down there somewhere. And anyway, who cared?

I spent most of my time in my "bedroom" with Snow, reading on my stomach or back. Sometimes I played with him. And often I carefully opened the air vent, took the binoculars, and looked through them at the Polish street across the wall. I felt as though I were living on a desert island. Instead of an ocean all around me there were people and buildings, but though they seemed close, they were really a world away. The binoculars were just a little pair of opera glasses. When I found them in the bunker I never dreamed that they would be worth as much as a good book, or even more.

It took a while, but after a couple of weeks I knew every grown-up and child in the Polish street. I knew who went to work early and who got up late. When the policeman worked the day shift, for example, he was always out of his house at the crack of dawn. Then came the mailman. The grocery and vegetable store opened early, too. The pharmacy opened much later, and the barber was last of all. But he also closed late. The doormen didn't all come out to sweep the sidewalks in front of their houses at the same time either. And they had different temperaments. There were those who liked to hit the peddlers, beggars, and old-clothes men who came around, and others who ignored them or even let them inside. Once I had thought that Polish doormen were mean to peddlers and old-clothes men because they were Jews. But these weren't Jews at all. At least no one thought they were, though I'll bet that some were in disguise.

For instance, the three little girls and the little boy who had straw-colored blond hair but Jewish eyes. I noticed them through my binoculars, of course. Once every week they appeared and went from courtyard to courtyard, or even stood in the street, singing songs. Mostly sad ones. People threw them coins wrapped in paper to make them easier to find among the cobblestones. There was one bearded doorman in a house on the corner who never let them into his yard. Whenever he saw them he cursed them and chased them as though they were stealing the bread from his mouth. Once he even shouted after them: "Kikes!" But they just stuck out their tongues at him and ran away.

And there was a woman who went every morning to the grocery and the vegetable store in a worn house-dress and tattered slippers. Her hair was uncombed and sometimes had pillow feathers in it. She was the wife of a drunkard. During the day he was nice enough. Sometimes he even played football with the children in the street. When he came home at night, though, often after the curfew had begun, he would holler and sing. I'll never know why the Germans didn't arrest him. Maybe he worked for them.

And then I'd hear curses and shrieks from the darkened windows of his house. And children crying. I'd bet anything that in the morning she'd show up with a black eye or at least a swollen lip.

It was a good thing that Jews didn't get drunk. What would I have done if I had a father who was nice during the day and a monster at night, like Dr. Jekyll and Mr. Hyde?

The couple who owned the grocery store were almost certainly dirty cheats. I couldn't hear what they said to their customers in the store, but children often came out of it crying. Sometimes grown-ups came out looking sad or annoyed too, or even waving a clenched fist at the storefront and swearing under their breaths. They thought that no one saw them. But I did. The fat vegetable man, on the other hand, was nice and usually friendly. Sometimes he'd give an apple to the hungry, dirty little girl who hung out all day long on the street. Her mother must have worked far away at some very hard job and had nowhere to leave her child; she always came home in the evening, right before the curfew, and left again, looking thin and pale, early the next day.

And then there was the bully who used to throw stones at us in the days before the transports. He still threw them at everything that moved, dogs, cats, and small children, and called everyone a "stinking kike." He knew lots of other swear words too, but those were his favorites. And he was the strongest boy in the neighborhood and bossed everyone around. For instance, when no one was looking he would pinch the little girl until she screamed and then act innocent. None of the other children in the street were his friends, but he told them all what to do and they did it, although they didn't want to. Whenever his aunt, who swore a blue streak herself, sent him on some errand, the children would play nicer games. They wouldn't hit or tease each other then, or throw stones. If ever I had to walk down that street, I knew I'd better watch out for him.

And there was a girl whom I liked very much. She reminded me a little of Martha, although she was older. She lived right across from me, and every evening before it got dark she sat down at the window, nibbling on her pencil or on the wooden handle of her pen, and did her homework. I envied her for going to school. Each morning I saw the children hurrying off to it with their schoolbags. Big ones and little ones. Sometimes the big ones held the little ones by the hand. And sometimes they'd run off and leave them until the little ones screamed and their mothers looked out the window and called to the big ones to come back.

One flight above the girl who did homework lived the crazy woman. She may not really have been crazy, but all day she did nothing but clean and dust and wipe and wash. The first thing in the morning she aired out all the bedclothes. Then she cleaned the window panes and scrubbed the windowsills. Next she took all her mattresses and blankets to the yard. I could see her leave her apartment with them and soon after I'd hear her beating them down below. I suppose she used the line that was meant for beating rugs. I couldn't see into the yard, though I was right across from its gate, because I was too high up.

After that she waxed and polished her floor until it gleamed. I could actually see the shine on it. It went on like that until noon, when she disappeared. Perhaps she lay down to rest. And then toward evening she appeared again at the gate, and if I hadn't had my binoculars I wouldn't have believed that she was the same crazy woman who had cleaned her house all day long, because now she was a fancy lady with lots of make-up who went off and didn't come back until the morning. It was really weird.

After I had been watching the street for about a month some new tenants moved in. They drove up in a large horse-drawn wagon and began to carry in their things. Every now and then they stopped to point angrily at the ghetto, as if to complain at having to live in cramped quarters when over there were whole streets of empty houses. I knew that it was just a matter of time before Poles came to live on our street. I didn't look forward to that. What would I do then? But as long as the Germans were still carting away the contents of the houses and shipping them to Germany, I knew that I had nothing to fear.

The newcomers were an old man and woman, a young woman, and three rough-looking young men — in other words, probably a husband and wife and four grown-up children. I was sure that they were crooks — looters, anyway. Often at night they crossed the wall with a ladder. I could hear them whispering. The policeman who lived next door to them must have known, but he never did anything about it. Maybe they paid him off. They would start with the houses near the wall and work their way through more distant ones, throwing what they had found over to the Polish side before climbing back over themselves. Once the Germans spotted them and opened fire. One of them fell and lay without moving, while another was dragged wounded through the front gate of the house.

I didn't feel sorry for them. I had even once seen one of

them hit his own mother. It was in the doorway of the grocery store. A second brother was standing by with his father. The old man shouted, but the brother did nothing. And another time, one evening before the curfew, I saw the three of them grab some man in the street and begin to beat him up. One of them pulled out a knife and would have killed him right there if a police patrol hadn't come by. They left the man and ran off — not into their house, somewhere else.

The brother who was wounded by the Germans was taken to the doctor. The doctor and his wife were no strangers to me either. They lived a flight below the girl who did homework. I could see right into his office with my binoculars. He was a real storybook doctor who patted children on the head and gave them candy. And the wounded crook, naturally, was brought to him. I couldn't see what happened next because of the blackout. But next day I saw the crook's mother crying in the doctor's office while he explained something to her and motioned with his hands. He pointed at the ghetto and tapped his head, as if to say: Isn't that the silliest thing you ever heard of, risking your life for some old rags! The mother talked too. She pressed her hands to her heart, but I couldn't guess what she said. Selling Jewish property was a good business for the Poles. And I suppose that it was just as well that they sold it, because that way at least the Germans didn't get it.

There was something else I saw too. Sometimes during curfew hours, either very late at night or very early in the morning, strangers would slip up to the same house and enter at the gate. I didn't know if it happened every night, because usually, unless I'd woken from a bad dream and not been able to doze off again, I was sleeping then. Those men didn't look like crooks to me. I thought they must belong to the Polish underground. At least that was my guess. They would tap a light rhythm on the gate, like the opening bar of a melody, and it would open at once. There was always a watchman there, either the doorman, his assistant, or his eldest daughter. And before the stranger was let in he had to whisper a password. Now and then the hinges of the gate were oiled to keep them from creaking. And once, when the doorman wouldn't open it because the taps weren't right, the visitor called in low tones, "To the doctor, governor." And the gate opened. Those words stuck in my head.

Once, in the middle of the day, a man was brought in a wagon. You couldn't tell at first that he was in it, because he was covered with sacks. But then the sacks were moved and, after making sure that there were no strangers in the street, his friends carefully lifted him out, laid him on a stretcher and hurried him inside. Only the bully was there, but that didn't seem to bother them.

When I wanted to know what time it was, I looked in the crazy woman's window. She had a big grandfather clock on the wall, which she didn't always remember to wind. And when she did, I didn't really have to look at it, because I could hear it chime every hour, half-hour, and quarter-hour.

I saw other things too that once, if I had just been running down the street, I would not have paid attention to. Things such as the old man who stole from the vegetable store, or the boy who used to pee in front of the pharmacy as soon as the druggist locked up. I watched the progress of the leaves, which had still been green when I moved in but had since turned slowly yellow and begun to fall. Autumn winds blew them up and down the sidewalks, and the doormen swore in the morning at the extra work. If it were up to me I'd have let them fly about, because they decorated the street like red and yellow butterflies. It was getting colder and colder. That didn't worry me, though. I had lots of clothing and quilts, and I could always light the burner and warm my hands over its flame. In daytime, I could even light it with an open vent.

Best of all I liked rainy days and thunderstorms. Then my larder seemed the safest, coziest place in the world. If the lightning bolts were in a part of the sky I could see, I'd watch them through the vent. There were always big ones that ripped through the sky. I told Snow that if you counted the seconds between the lightning and the thunderclap, and then multiplied them by three hundred and thirty, you'd get the distance in meters that the lightning was from you. He was such a dumb mouse that I had to explain that the reason was that light reached us immediately, while sound traveled at a speed of three hundred and thirty meters per second.

I wished that there were a boy my own age in one of those houses whom I could invite to visit. Or that I could telephone the girl who did homework, so that we could get to know each other.

The bully teased her, too. Sometimes he started up with her in the morning when she was on her way to school. He never went to school himself. He must have been kicked out of lots of them. But he didn't pick on her the way he did on the others. He never pinched her or tripped her, for instance, or stood in her way until she cried. It was a whole different thing.

At first it worried me. I didn't understand what he wanted from her. I thought that in the end he'd beat her up the way he did everyone else, boy or girl, big or small — unless, of course, they were bigger than him. After a while, though, I stopped worrying and started getting annoyed. Sometimes I felt I could have killed him. He would bow to her, sweeping the sidewalk with his cap and saying all kinds of things that I couldn't hear, because it was a noisy time of day, but that she didn't find the least bit funny. Sometimes he would plant himself in front of her and wait for her to scold him before he moved. And yet though he pestered her, he did it with a strange kind of politeness. Maybe he was sweet on her like I was. I guess that's what made me so mad.

Sometimes I didn't feel like reading or playing with Snow or even looking at the Polish side of the wall. All of a sudden I'd start thinking about father and mother. I never cried, but I'd lie in the larder thinking about all the terrible things that could happen, and about how lucky the Polish kids were for having homes and being able to play where they wanted. Except that then I'd remember the other children who had been in the factory with me and realize that I had no right to complain. Not as long as I was here, waiting for my father.

 **13**

The Uprising

Suddenly one morning I heard people being marched through the street to the depot. It was scary. A lot of them, group after group, just like when Ghettos B and C were cleared out. It went on for two days. I didn't dare try to look. The footsteps would come nearer, pass the front gate, and grow fainter again. Now and then a child cried or screamed.

And then, early on the morning of the third day, just when the crazy woman began shaking out her blankets, I heard shots. At first I hardly noticed them. But they grew louder. They stopped and started up again farther away. Then they stopped and started up nearer. It kept on like that. The bully ran in the street, shouting, "They're finishing off the kikes! They're finishing off the kikes!"

I couldn't make out what anyone else on the Polish side was saying. It was too bad that my binoculars didn't have an amplifier. But from the shots and the snatches of conversation that reached me, I understood that there was a Jewish uprising. Finally. It made me proud. I took out my pistol and wondered if I should leave my hideout and join it. What if father should come? Yet I had a weapon and should go. I took Yossi's little shoulder bag and put into it a bottle of water and as much food as would fit. I also packed my big kitchen knife. I'd have to wait for it to get dark, because I could never reach Ghetto A in broad daylight. And I'd have to say good-bye to Snow. If I survived, I'd come back and look for him in the ruins. There was no way I could take him with me. I'd have to run and crawl and hide in cellars and lofts, and he'd just get crushed in my pocket.

When everything was ready I went to the house next door as I did every morning. As usual I hoisted the ladder back up from below. I was careful never to leave it down even for a minute: That was an ironclad law, as was always taking the pistol with me. Suddenly shots broke out in the street nearby. I heard shouts and automatic fire. Then single shots. And people running. And more shots. Had the revolt spread? I didn't know if that was good or bad. Maybe it was bad for the rebels. But for me it was good, because if the fighting had reached Bird Street, I wouldn't have to wait for the evening to be part of it.

I was slipping back through the passage when two men burst into Number 78 and climbed onto the ruins. One was wounded. He held his arm and had blood on his shirt. The second, who looked very pale, supported him. They stopped and glanced frantically around them, looking for a place to hide. Neither was armed. They were still getting their bearings when a German soldier ran in after them. He raised his rifle, aimed it at them, and shouted, *"Halt!"*

They froze and put up their hands. The soldier laughed. I knew that laugh. It was a bad sign. I took out my pistol.

My mind felt blank. I acted without thinking. It was as though someone else were moving for me and telling me what to do. The soldier cocked his rifle. Just then he slipped on a loose brick and I cocked my pistol too. You can't hear a safety catch being released. I aimed at him while he aimed again at them, and then I fired quickly three times, one shot after another. The two men hit the ground. They must have thought that the soldier had shot at them and missed. One of them pulled out a knife and ran toward him like a lunatic. As if he could have reached him if he had been alive! Suddenly he stopped short, still without grasping what had happened. They couldn't see me from where they were standing.

The soldier had a helmet on. His uniform was green. He still had a look of surprise on his face when he spun around and fell. The rifle dropped slowly from his hands. He dropped to the ground slowly too, like a rag doll. His body shuddered slightly once or twice, as though trying to finish its laugh.

I stepped out of the passageway. The shots in the street were growing fainter. Then they could no longer be heard. One thing was for sure, we had better hide fast. And we had better hide the dead German too.

The young man put his knife away. He noticed me for the first time but ignored me, ran to the German, and grabbed his rifle. Then he stripped off his cartridge belt. I remained where I was. I had already seen enough.

"Hey, you, who shot him?" gasped the wounded man.

"Shhh, be quiet," said his friend. He turned to me and asked, "Did you see who shot the soldier?"

"I shot him," I said.

"Son," said the man severely, "did you understand what I asked you?"

I nodded. He repeated the question.

"Yes," I said, nodding again. I showed them the pistol and stuck it quickly back into my pocket before they could get any ideas about it.

They gave me an unbelieving look.

"We'd better find somewhere to hide fast," said the wounded man.

"Where is your hiding place?" asked his friend. "Do you have room for us there?"

I didn't answer. I just went over to the frayed wire and pulled hard. The ladder fell to the ground. I pointed to it. They didn't hesitate. The wounded man tried climbing it first but couldn't make it.

"Do you have a rope?" asked his friend.

I climbed up and threw him one down.

"Go get a grown-up!"

"There's no one here but me," I said.

He tied the rope to his friend and climbed up first; then we both pulled the wounded man after us. I warned them not to pass in front of the window. I quickly drew up the ladder and the three of us lay down on the floor. I wanted to bring water, but they wouldn't let me. They didn't realize that we couldn't be seen. And maybe a standing grown-up was visible from the gate. I had no way of knowing.

"They won't find us here," whispered the wounded man.

"If they find that soldier, though . . ." said his friend without finishing his thought.

They grew aware of the noises and shouts on the Polish side, and I explained to them what they were. I don't know if we lay there for five minutes or half an hour. Finally I began to talk. I told them that we couldn't be seen and that I had food and water. I asked if they had been in the uprising.

"No," said the wounded man's friend. "We tried reaching it. A Pole in the underground got us into the ghetto, and we were on our way to the fighting when we ran into a patrol. There were ten of us. Not all of us were armed. If only I'd had this rifle half an hour ago . . ." He sighed.

"Bolek told us not to take any short cuts, but Shmulik insisted," said the wounded man. And he added, "It's bleeding again."

"Who's Bolek?" I asked.

"The Pole," said the wounded man. "Our Polish liaison."

"Do you have any bandages?" his friend asked me.

"No," I said.

I remembered the case with the red cross in the house next door and told them about it. But I didn't know if it was still there, and in any case it was too dangerous to try to get it. I opened the larder, took out a sheet and a knife, and began to cut the sheet into strips. The wounded man lay groaning. His friend stared into the larder with wide eyes.

"Who else lives up here?" he asked.

"No one," I said again.

He frowned. He must have thought that I wasn't telling him the truth because I was afraid he might rat or something.

"What do you take us for?" he asked angrily.

"If I didn't trust you," I said, "I wouldn't have taken you up here."

"Then you're really here by yourself?"

Now it was my turn to be angry. I ripped off a big strip of sheet with my hand instead of cutting it with the knife.

"Stop making so much noise," said the wounded man's friend.

His name was Freddy. The wounded man was Henryk.

Freddy bandaged Henryk's wound. Then the two of us helped him lie down on my bed in the larder. He drank thirstily. Freddy drank, too. They weren't hungry, though. They had eaten before setting out.

"We have to get rid of the soldier," said Freddy. "They must not have seen him run in here. They haven't missed him yet."

"I'll help you," I said.

We climbed down. I yanked the wire and the ladder rose in the air and hung over the bottom floor. I felt like a snake charmer. Then I let the wire go and it dropped out of sight.

"Did you figure that out by yourself?" Freddy asked.

I nodded.

"Who built you this hideout?"

"I built it myself. I've been living here for two months."

"I don't believe it."

"Then don't."

Freddy stripped off the German soldier's uniform. I tried not to look.

"I need his clothes," he apologized.

He wrapped them up with the helmet and hid them behind a pile of bricks. Then he grabbed the German's legs and dragged him over the ruins to the passageway where he had first seen me.

"Get rid of any signs of him," he told me.

I covered the puddle of blood and the dead man's and Freddy's tracks with broken plaster and bricks.

It took all our strength to get the soldier through the passageway. It amazed me how little I cared that he was dead.

"Now what?" I asked.

"We'll dump him in one of the apartments," said Freddy.

"But I live next door," I said. "You can't leave a dead soldier here. He'll be found and they'll come."

Freddy laid the soldier on the floor and said, "Now that I have a rifle and bullets, I'll join the uprising tonight. But Henryk will stay with you. His wound isn't serious. The bullet can be gotten out. And he knows how to cross to the Polish side. We have a liaison there, and he'll get hold of his address. The liaison will help both of you to reach the resistance in the forests. There's no point in your staying on here by yourself. Not that your hideout isn't fantastic. I still can hardly believe that you made it yourself. But you have to realize that the ghetto will soon be opened to Poles. What will you do then? You won't be able to move. You won't even be able to breathe. Especially if someone tries squatting in these ruins. You know, they have a terrible housing shortage. Someone's liable to build a hut or a cabin in here."

"I can't leave," I said.

It was clear to me that I wasn't going anywhere. Not even to join the uprising as I had thought this morning. I realized now that real wars weren't like the ones in adventure books where children fought like heroes at the grownups' sides. One dead German soldier on the floor was enough for me. I would stay here.

"But why can't you?"

"I'm waiting for my father."

"Does he know you're here?"

"Yes."

"When is he coming?"

I shrugged. "Where is he?"

"I don't know. They took him the day they closed our factory."

"Which factory was that?"

"The rope factory."

He started to say something and stopped. "We'll talk about it later," he declared after a pause. He looked at me strangely, and then added, "Go back to your hideout. I'll throw him in the garbage dump in the yard and cover him as best I can. There's certainly enough junk to do it with."

"Maybe I'd better stand lookout at the gate," I said.

He looked doubtful. "All right. But you're as white as a sheet."

"I feel fine," I said, touching my face in surprise.

I went to stand at the gate of the house next door. The street was deserted. From time to time I heard explosions and volleys of rifle fire in the distance. It was the uprising.

It took Freddy a long time, or so it seemed. All of a sudden I didn't feel so good. What was wrong with me? It wasn't as though I'd been afraid. Could I be getting sick?

Freddy finally finished and called to me. "Well, that's that," he said, slapping me on the shoulder. We slipped back through the passageway. I jerked the wire and the ladder fell to the ground.

"You were talking before about a Pole named Bolek," I said. "What does he look like?"

"First, let's climb back up. Are you sure that you feel all right?"

Actually, I wasn't. I felt as though something were shaking inside, and the shaking kept getting worse. We climbed up and I pulled the ladder after us. Freddy described Bolek for me. Now I was sure of it: He was the same man as the one I had met. I understood now how a looter could have been so nice. He must have just made believe he was collecting those suits. I didn't say anything, though. I just repeated his address to myself.

And then I burst out crying. I couldn't keep it in anymore. It was too much for me. All at once it burst from my throat. Freddy hugged me against him as hard as he could and stroked my head. Maybe it was all those tears wanting out that had made me so pale and trembly. It took me a long while to stop, though I tried to cry as quietly as I could.

I had remembered father's lesson well. I had done everything with technical proficiency exactly as he had taught me, without thinking or feeling a thing. Cocking the gun. Holding it steady. Releasing the safety catch. Aligning the sights with the target. Never hesitating for a moment. Thoughts and feelings were for afterward. If you had them while aiming, your hand would shake. And then you would be the one to die.

I kept trying to stop crying but could not. Yet how had I been any different from Robinson Crusoe? Robinson had also shot the savages when they had tried to eat Friday.

I cooked rice for the two of them and opened the last can of evaporated milk in their honor. Freddy changed Henryk's bandage, and they whispered between them, glancing at me from time to time. I guessed Freddy was telling Henryk to convince me to go to the forests with him.

I showed Freddy the larder on the top floor and he climbed up and went to sleep in it for the rest of the day. I passed the time on the bottom floor chatting with Henryk. I was sorry now that I hadn't taken the chess set from the bunker. We made a checkerboard from some white cardboard and used coins and pieces of wood for the men. I even beat him a few times. Maybe he lost to me on purpose. And then again, maybe he didn't.

Freddy left us in the evening. He shook Henryk's hand. I wanted to shake his hand too, but instead he hugged and kissed me hard. Then he took the German's uniform and put the helmet on his head. He smiled and saluted, as though he were already a real soldier, and disappeared into the darkness. I listened to his footsteps pass through the ruins and out the front gate.

All night long I kept being woken by Henryk's groans and the sound of shots far away. I wondered if they were Freddy's, and I prayed for him.

14

To the Doctor

Henryk's groans woke me early. He was feeling very bad and had a fever. In fact, he was burning up. He was obviously in no shape to go anywhere. He could hardly even speak, though he tried to in order to reassure me. I gave him some water to drink. He couldn't sit up, so I had to spoon it slowly into his mouth as if he were a baby. I thought he was going to die and decided I had to get a doctor. The only doctor I knew, though, had never seen me in his life. I asked Henryk how his group had crossed the wall. He told me that there was a secret passage in a house on the corner of Bird and Bakers streets. He talked very slowly, either because he wanted to make sure I understood or else because he couldn't talk faster. I wet a towel and laid it on his forehead. That made him feel a little better. Mother used to do the same thing for me whenever I had a fever.

"Thirty-two Bakers Street," Henryk whispered again.

I looked out the air vent at the Polish street. The children hadn't left for school yet. But the bully was already outside, looking for a victim. The little girl was nowhere to be seen. The only person to torment was the crazy woman, who was shaking out her pillows and sheets. He called up to her, "Hey, lady, you dropped a pillow!"

She leaned over to have a look and went back to work. He seemed disappointed. Was he really so stupid that he thought she'd run right down? Perhaps. The policeman came out and shook his fist at him. Everyone knew him. He threw a big rock at an innocent dog passing by. The dog yelped. The doctor's wife looked out the window and started to scold him. Just then his aunt appeared and screamed, "Haven't you gone yet? How can you hang around here like that when I told you to be on your way?! Where's the note?"

"I've got it," he shouted, taking a piece of paper from his pocket and waving it at her.

"Then get going, you lazy bum!"

She was sending him on some errand, as usual. I kept him in sight as long as I could. I guessed he'd be gone for a while. I studied the doctor's office through my binoculars. He was in. His wife brought him some tea, and he sat drinking it and writing at his desk.

I took a flashlight with me but not the pistol. I couldn't use it anyway, even if some Polish kids caught me. I'd just have to take my chances without it.

"If my father comes," I told Henryk, "he'll call 'Alex.' "

"Take some money," he murmured, pointing to his pocket.

I took some bills from it and left the larder open a crack so that he could hear. Then I chose clothes. I knew exactly how children my age dressed when they went to school. I took a few books and notebooks and tied them with a belt, the way poor kids who had no schoolbags did. Last of all, I put on the beat-up Polish soldier's hat and jammed it down over my eyes. Bakers Street was the last street to cross Bird Street before the factory. I knew the way well. There were no looters to worry about at this time of day, and the only thing to watch out for was Germans emptying houses. But though I hadn't actually checked, it seemed to me that the houses on our side of the street had already all been gone through.

I knew that Number 32 bordered on the ghetto wall, yet it had never occurred to me that there might be a passage there, not even when I met Bolek in the house around the corner from it. I climbed down to its cellar and followed Henryk's directions to the third storage room on the left. It was dark. I lit the flashlight but couldn't find anything. I felt the walls with my hand. And then I decided to move a broken chest of drawers away from a wall. Henryk had said clearly, "You'll see some loose bricks there." And I did, right behind the chest. I began to remove them one by one. Not all of them, though, because the passage seemed to have been made for very fat men. A small hole was all I needed.

I replaced all the bricks behind me. I was in a small, dark space now. I shone my flashlight and found an opening that was blocked from the outside. I pushed hard. Nothing gave. It must have been a heavy piece of furniture. I shoved again with all my strength. It rasped on the floor and I squeezed through.

I was in the cellar of another house on the Polish side of the wall. I prayed that no one would come down now for coal or potatoes from the storage room. I stood still for a moment, listening. Up above I heard children. A woman shouted. A man answered her. I climbed to the ground floor and walked through the front gate without looking to see if the doorman was watching me. There had been no need to cross the courtyard, because the doorway was right by the gate. This was odd, because most houses weren't like that. I tried to look ordinary. Of course, the doorman had only to look at me to know that I didn't live there. Maybe he knew about the passage and didn't bother anyone. It was hard to believe that you could keep such a thing from a doorman.

I walked along the wall on the Polish side, heading back toward Number 78. I passed a grocery store that wasn't mine — I mean that wasn't the one facing my hideout — and couldn't resist going in to buy a roll. The grocer changed a bill for me. I had better learn what things cost. I had a terrible craving for some milk too, but I knew that I mustn't overdo it. A real hot roll! I walked along eating it with open pleasure. A few children, the first off to school, were already in the street. Some paid me no attention. Others stared at me, because they were seeing me for the first time. I ignored them. Let them think I was new in the neighborhood. What could they possibly suspect?

I reached the doctor's house. It was really a short walk. When I had covered the same distance on the ghetto side, traveling through lofts and passages between houses, climbing up and down stairs, it had seemed at least twice as long, even without the stops to listen on the way.

I was opposite my hideout now. Number 78 looked deserted. Even a little frightening. It was funny to think that if I were looking out of my air vent now I'd see myself walking in the Polish street. The lower part of the building was hidden by the ghetto wall, but I could see the top of the second-floor window and the four windows above it. They all looked empty, just like the windows of all the other houses on the street. My air vent couldn't be seen, perhaps because it was in shadow.

I approached the gate of the doctor's house. It was closed as usual. I didn't try to tap the right rhythm. I just knocked on it.

The doorman opened it slightly. "Yes?"

Now I could see him close up. His mustache was really big and waxed, just like I'd thought it was. He didn't frighten me at all. And I knew just what to say.

"To the doctor, governor."

He regarded me and my belted books with curious amazement and let me pass.

When I knocked on the doctor's door my heart began to pound. What would I say to him? I hadn't given it any thought. I read the white sign that said:

DR. STANISLAW POLAWSKI

DOCTOR OF INTERNAL MEDICINE

"Helinka," I heard him call from an inner room. "There's someone at the door."

His wife's slippers padded toward the door. It opened wide. It had no safety chain.

"What is it, boy? Aren't you late for school? Did something happen at home?"

I took off my hat and stepped into the hallway. She clapped her hands and exclaimed, "Jesus, look at your hair! Is that how you go to school? With a head like that?"

I didn't answer.

"Well, what is it that you want?"

I still didn't answer.

"Did something happen to your father or mother? Or to one of your brothers? Why were you sent here?"

"I have to talk to the doctor, ma'am," I whispered.

I hadn't meant to whisper. It just came out that way. Suddenly I realized that my wild head of hair would give me away whenever I took off my hat. The doctor's wife led me into his office. I said nothing until she closed the door. The doctor stared at my hair too but made no comment. Well, if I seemed suspicious to him, it should help make him believe me. I looked out the window at Number 78. Henryk was so close.

"Doctor," I said, pointing, "over there, where that window is, is a man who was wounded in the Jewish uprising. He has a bullet in his shoulder that has to be taken out."

The doctor turned to look at the empty shell of a house. Then he turned back to me and asked, "How do you know?"

"Sir, I've been hiding out in that house for a long time myself. I know a way to get there that's pretty safe. I've just come by it. You have to come with me. Please, sir. He's burning with fever."

"How am I supposed to believe a story like that? Maybe you were sent here by some . . . some . . ."

He didn't finish the sentence. He didn't seem to want to.

"Did the doorman let you in?"

"Yes. I said, 'To the doctor, governor.' "

"Who told you to say that?"

I began to tell him the whole story from the beginning.

"Sit down," he interrupted me when I was halfway through. "Would you like anything to eat?"

"Just some milk," I said.

He called his wife. They whispered together for a minute. Even before she gave me the milk, she brought some barber's shears. She wrapped a sheet around my neck and the doctor cut my hair like an expert while I went on with my story. Someone came to see him, but he said that he had no time because he had to go at once to visit a critically ill patient. He excitedly gathered all his things while his wife swept up my fallen hair. There really was a big pile of it.

"Do you have any water there?"

"Yes. Straight from the tap."

"Incredible," he murmured to himself as his wife helped him on with his coat. "Incredible."

I didn't tell him about the German or the pistol. I was too embarrassed.

His wife tried putting some food for me into his case but there wasn't any room. In the end I took three apples. One of them I ate and the other two I stuck in my pocket.

On our way out we met the girl who did homework coming down the stairs. I must have blushed but I managed to say, "Good morning."

She stopped for a second and looked at me carefully, as if trying to place me. She couldn't, of course, but she smiled and said good morning back to me before running on down the stairs two steps at a time.

"Do you know her?" asked the doctor.

"No," I said. "But I see her from my air vent whenever she sits down to do her homework."

"She's a very nice girl," he said.

I didn't doubt that, but I kept silent. There were four people now who knew about my hideout: Freddy, if he was still alive, Henryk, and the doctor and his wife. Not counting father and Boruch, of course.

I took off my hat and felt my hair. It was short and prickly.

"Were you ever a barber?" I asked.

"Once, in the army," he laughed.

It was my luck that I had found a little scissors in an empty apartment with which I could at least trim my nails. At first I only trimmed them on my left hand because I could only work the scissors with my right. After a while, though, I learned to work them with my left hand too. At home there used to be a big fight every time I had to cut my nails until I agreed to let mother bring the scissors. If grandmother was visiting, she would collect the trimmings in a piece of paper and burn them in the oven. Because otherwise your soul would have to wander about looking for them for a long time after you died.

I think grandmother really believed that. Why would she have collected them so carefully if she hadn't?

15

The Operation

The doorman knew the doctor. He doffed his hat, bowed to him, and checked to make sure we weren't being followed before taking us down to the cellar. I guessed he must have been in the underground, too, because nobody had asked him to come with us. He moved the chest of drawers and replaced it as soon as we entered the dark space behind it. I turned on my flashlight and removed some loose bricks. This time I had to take out more of them. The doctor helped me put them back.

I led him from house to house, through lofts and walls. I was glad that we didn't have to cross any roofs, because it wasn't easy to balance on the chimney sweeps' planks that ran above the steep tiles. By now I was an expert at it, but the doctor was no longer young. From time to time he had to catch his breath. At first, I pretended that we had to stop to listen anyway, but after a while I saw that he wasn't ashamed of having to rest. Maybe it's only boys who don't like to admit when they're tired. Except that I remember how my Uncle Robert, who was short-winded, always did his best to hide it, too.

We reached Number 78. It was quiet. I lowered the ladder. Henryk was too weak to look out and see who was there.

In no time the doctor had recovered and was as brisk and efficient as could be. He opened a bandage, laid his instruments on a towel spread on a wooden board, and stuck a rag in Henryk's mouth to keep him from biting his tongue or his lips. Then he opened the wound and cleaned it thoroughly. I helped as best I could. He was worried that all the blood would scare me, but it didn't. I hadn't told him that I'd always planned to be a doctor when I grew up. Now, after getting to know him, I was sure that I wanted to be a doctor.

Henryk kept squirming from the pain. The doctor gave him some vodka to drink.

"We'll make him a little tipsy," he said, smiling at me. "Are you all right?"

That was the same thing Freddy had asked me after I killed the German.

"Do I look pale?" I asked.

"No," he said. "You look fine."

He began to operate. With a special pincers he pulled out the bullet as neatly as though he had been doing it all his life and held it triumphantly up.

"Here, have a look."

Henryk passed out.

"That's good," said the doctor. "Much better than anesthesia."

He poured lots of iodine into the wound. I held the bandage for him and he put it on Henryk. He showed me how to change it, gave me some bandages, iodine, and aspirins, and shut his case.

Henryk came to. We helped him back into the larder and

I closed the doors. First, though, the doctor wanted to look at his house through the air vent. To see it through my eyes.

He smiled and patted me on the shoulder. I walked him all the way back. This time I took the pistol with me. I couldn't resist showing it to him. It was the first time I'd boasted about it to anyone. It felt good to see how impressed he was. I'll bet no other boy in the whole city had a gun like me. No other Polish boy, anyway.

"Well, have you killed anyone with it yet?" he joked.

You couldn't tell it had been shot from looking at it. I had cleaned it well and oiled it with cooking oil. I didn't answer. Suddenly I felt uncomfortable. After all, he was a doctor. It was only when we sat down to rest after having struggled through a particularly hard passage that I told him what had happened.

"People shouldn't kill each other, son," he said, speaking slowly and very seriously. "People should help each other to live. Killing human beings is the most terrible of crimes, although unfortunately it's become a common one lately. But if you're saving the life of a friend or someone in your family, or defending your country, or just trying to keep yourself alive, there's nothing to be ashamed of. It's no disgrace to kill a murderer like the soldier you told me about. On the contrary, I think you were very brave. I want you to know that, just in case no one's told you yet."

All at once he bent down and kissed me. Then we continued on our way.

"I'll come back to check our patient in two days," he said. "Meet me at the passage at this exact time of day. But wait for me there. Don't cross over to look for me."

"All right," I said. "I'll see you leaving your house in the morning, and I'll come to meet you."

"If the operation succeeded, so much the better. But if by any chance the wound has gotten infected, we'll have to get your friend to an experienced nurse. Let's hope that he'll be all right."

We said good-bye.

That night I heard only a few scattered shots from Ghetto A, and the next day there was nothing. Heavy clouds of smoke arose from it and hung over the city. When night came again we could see the glow of flames. The ghetto was burning. Maybe they'd set fire to it on purpose to smoke the Jewish fighters out.

In the morning Henryk felt better. He ate some potatoes and one of the apples I had brought. I had kept them both for him. I showed him Snow and put him through his paces. Snow performed all his tricks. He came to me when I whistled and went off to hunt for his breakfast when I whistled again. Henryk couldn't get over him. He had never had a pet mouse when he was a boy. He had had a big Siamese cat.

I told him about myself, my parents, and how I came to Number 78. Then he told me about himself. He thought his whole family was dead. He had no hope of meeting anyone after the war the way I did. We talked about what would be then. Not just about walking wherever we pleased, or hiking in the country, or boating, or skating and skiing in the winter, but about things that mother used to talk about too. About Palestine. Henryk called it *"Erets Yisra'el."*

He talked about the Jews, whose whole problem was that

they had no country of their own, and about *Erets Yisra'el.*
He lay there with his eyes shut and talked on and on, as
though he were delirious and could actually see the Jewish
state that we would have one day, with a flag and a presi-
dent of its own. Of course, I would have preferred a king,
but I didn't interrupt to tell him that. It was strange to think
of a whole city being Jewish. You'd walk down a street, for
instance, and everyone you saw would be a Jew: the taxi
drivers and the coachmen, the porters and the mailmen, the
chimney sweeps and the policemen, the children and the
doormen — Jews, every last one of them. No one would
have to be afraid to go outside because he had a Jewish face
and big, sad Jewish eyes. No one would make fun of him or
pick on him. No one would laugh or say he had a Jewish
nose.

"What will our national anthem be?" I asked.

"Don't you know it?" asked Henryk in amazement.

"No," I said. "My mother never mentioned it."

He began to sing in a low voice. And I did know it. It was
a melody that mother had once sung me to sleep with.

The next morning I woke up in a fright. I had heard a car
drive up quickly and screech to a stop. It sounded like the
Gestapo. But it wasn't in the ghetto. It was on the Polish
side.

I stepped carefully over Henryk, who was breathing
heavily in his sleep, and opened the air vent. The car had
pulled up in front of the house across from us. I didn't have
to worry about the girl. But the doctor was something else.
Two policemen ran inside. A third remained by the wheel.
They wore Gestapo uniforms. Had someone ratted? It was

always the same story. The rats should all have been killed before the war. Only how could you have known then who they'd be?

The policemen came down with the doctor and pushed him into the car. He was wearing his coat, but I could see his pajama bottoms beneath it. It was strange to see him without his doctor's case, because I'd always seen him with it until now. It made him look like a different man.

From then on the curtains in the window of his office remained closed. His wife vanished too, and I never saw her again. I just hoped to God it wasn't because of me. Or because of Henryk. And most likely it wasn't. Sometimes people in the underground simply got caught, the same as with Jews.

16
Bolek

Henryk wasn't well. And he was getting worse. I didn't think it was because of the wound. That seemed to be healing well. A scab was forming and his arm hardly hurt him at all. He was simply sick. Maybe he had typhus or something. He kept losing consciousness. And when he recovered it, he would see me double or not recognize me at all. At night he talked out loud to himself. That was awfully scary. I'd try covering his mouth with my hand or waking him. He wouldn't awaken, but he would quiet down for a while. I was afraid to sleep. I made him hot tea and put cold compresses on his forehead. And I had to keep bringing him rags from the house next door, because he couldn't get up to go to the bathroom.

It went on like that for three weeks. And then, slowly, he began to get better. He was still as weak as a fly and could hardly talk. But at least we were done with the rags. He could use a pot now. Sometimes he hugged me and whispered how wonderful I was for having saved his life. That embarrassed me. I mean, I had saved it all right, but why make a big deal of it?

One day, when he was able to stand and climb down the rope ladder, I told him that I knew where to find Bolek, the Polish liaison who had gotten him into the ghetto on the first day of the uprising.

"How do you know?"

I told him that, too.

"Give me his address," he said. "I'll go there."

I laughed. Henryk didn't just look like a Jew; he looked like a Jew to end all Jews. Besides which, he was still sick and weak.

"I'll go talk to him," I said.

I thought a lot about the best time to go. I preferred not to be on the Polish side again when the children went to school. I wasn't sure how long it would take me to find Bolek, and I didn't want to be the only boy in the street on my way back. But neither did I want to be around when school let out and everyone let off steam after having been cooped up all day long in the classroom. Not that I would have minded letting off a little steam myself — but I knew that that was the time when boys most often looked for trouble and got others into it.

I decided on the afternoon. I'd take a shopping basket with me. In fact, it would give me a chance to buy a few groceries. I took some money from Henryk. He insisted on giving me more than I wanted.

"You never know," he said.

On my way to Number 32 I searched through several apartments until, in the corner of one, I found a basket and a pitcher for milk. Stuff like that wasn't worth sending to Germany.

The entrance to Number 32 hadn't changed, but this

time the doorman stopped me at the gate. What did he want from me? Didn't he remember who I was? It turned out that he remembered very well.

"The first time you were here," he said, "you ran past me before I could stop you, and I didn't feel like chasing after you. The second time you came with the doctor. That's why there wasn't any charge. But this time you either pay me or go back. You Jews always have money."

Now I understood how the looters got in and out of the ghetto. And I understood too why the loose bricks made such a large hole. It wasn't for very fat people. It was my good luck that Henryk had made me take the extra money. It had saved me another trip.

"How much is it?"

He claimed he was giving me a children's discount. I paid and passed through the gate. The one good thing about it was that I didn't have to be afraid of him anymore. At least now I knew where I stood with him. I made a mental note to ask Henryk for some money when he left so that I could cross over again if I had to and buy a few things now and then.

Once more I was on the Polish side. This time, though, I wasn't in a rush the way I was when I went for the doctor. I felt more sure of myself too — and that, according to father, was what counted the most. Instead of taking the shortest route, I decided to make a detour through the park. I walked slowly, as though I were out for a stroll. But come to think of it, I really was. Why hadn't I done it before? So far, even if this was only my second time on the Polish side, not one single person had taken me for a Jew.

I felt drunk. I had almost forgotten the reason I had

come. The park looked like it always did in autumn. The leaves lay thick on the ground and still fell from some trees, while others were already bare and ready for snow. Mothers wheeled babies in carriages. Or maybe they were governesses. There must still be people rich enough to afford them. Children pedaled their bicycles and rolled hoops with sticks or metal rods. That was something I had never learned to do. Maybe I had just been too small for it.

Some boys my own age were playing football. I watched them shout and fight as they chose sides. It was always like that. One of the captains pointed to me and said that his team needed a goalie. I was always good at keeping goal and there really was no hurry, so I stayed for the game. And I didn't let my team down.

"Where do you live?" asked the captain.

"Will you come again tomorrow?" asked another boy.

"You bet!" I said.

Luckily it started to rain and everyone ran home. I put the empty shopping basket on my head and ran too. I passed the grocery across from my hideout and stepped into it, hoping the girl might be there. But there was only one other customer. I asked for milk, ten eggs, and some bread, making sure to say first, "My mother told me to get . . ." I almost asked for rolls too. I caught myself just in time. Rolls were only in the morning. Milk was usually bought in the morning, too, but there still was some left. I looked to see what the woman in front of me paid for her groceries and then paid for mine with Henryk's money. The grocer gave me change. I didn't count it, so as not to annoy him. Then I waited a while in the store for the rain to stop.

It was almost winter. The past week such strong winds

had blown that you could hear the trees creak on the Polish side of the wall. The ground in the park had felt frozen beneath my feet. But the cold didn't bother me in the larder. My one worry was that I'd run out of kerosene and not be able to make "tea." That was Henryk's word, too, for the hot water that we sipped through cubes of sugar held in our mouths.

"Are you new around here?" asked the grocer.

"Yes," I said. "We moved in last week."

"You don't say!" he said. "I saw you go by here one morning."

"I was on my way to the doctor," I said.

He let out a sigh. Something about it sounded phony to me.

"The poor man," he said. "He had a heart of gold. And what a doctor he was! Those informers. What did you say your address was?"

I didn't have to answer, because just then two women and the bully entered the store. The bully sized me up right away. I saw now that he wasn't as tall as he had seemed from the air vent. Maybe that was because the other children were even smaller. On my way out he tried tripping me.

"You cut that out!" said one of the women. "Let's have none of your tricks now."

It was his aunt, the one who was always shouting from the window: "Yanek, you bum, shake a leg!"

And he would answer: "I'm coming, Aunt Kristina!" But he would stay right where he was.

"A new boy," said the grocer to his customers as I opened the door.

I hurried into the street before they had a chance to find out that I was lying and that no new family had moved in. I mustn't come here anymore. From now on I'd do my shopping at the grocery near Bakers Street, where I'd bought the roll on my way to the doctor. The owners there were nicer, and I could cross right back to the ghetto if I had to. The doorman could be counted on, too. I wasn't sure how much he'd help me, but he certainly wouldn't turn me in. He made a living from people like me.

The rain was mixed with sleet now. I turned up my collar, pulled my hat down over my ears, and began to run again. Suddenly I bumped into a boy coming toward me and knocked him down. I put down my basket and helped him to his feet.

"I'm sorry," I said. "It wasn't on purpose."

It wasn't a boy. It was the girl. She'd banged her knee hard and looked like she was going to cry. But she didn't. She recognized me right away and did her best to smile.

"Oh, it's you," she said. "Did you know that they took the doctor?"

"Yes," I said. We moved closer to the wall of the building to get out of the rain. "My name's Alex," I said.

"Mine's Stashya. Brrr, it's cold." Her teeth were chattering.

I wanted so badly to tell her about myself. And about how I watched her through the air vent. But I'd never be able to. At least not until the end of the war. And then, red with embarrassment, I asked, "Would you like to be friends?"

"You're kidding me."

"No," I said. "I mean it."

"All right," she said. "But I have to run home now. Are you new around here?"

"I live across the park," I said. "Would you like to meet me there? I sometimes go there to play football."

"Kids laugh when they see a boy and a girl together."

"We'll find a place where no one will see us."

"Tomorrow?"

"I can't," I said.

I had no way of knowing what would happen. Whether or not I'd find Bolek now, for instance, or when Henryk would leave. Not that I couldn't cross over if he stayed. Except that he might not want me to. He might say that it was too dangerous. Well, what if he did? The danger didn't scare me. At most, I'd leave him the pistol. No, I wouldn't. It was mine.

"Come to the park next Monday," I told her. "You know, in the afternoon. The same time as now. Unless it rains."

"And if it snows?"

"Snow is fine," I said.

We said good-bye and ran off in different directions. I turned left at the corner and soon found Bolek's house. It wasn't far. It really was on the same street that we took before the war on our way to grandmother's house.

I entered at the gate. A teenager guarding it looked suspiciously at me and my basket.

"Where does Bolek live?" I asked nonchalantly.

"Where do you think?" he sneered, pointing to the doorman's quarters by the gate.

I really had asked a dumb question. I knocked on the door. The doorman answered. It was Bolek, except that now he was wearing a uniform and heavy boots. At first he didn't recognize me. I took off my wet hat and politely said hello. And then he remembered.

"Ah, Alex!" he exclaimed. "Come in." His wife was inside. I hesitated. "Speak up," he said. "What's wrong?"

At first I couldn't get myself to talk. He took me into the apartment and shut the door. And then it all came out at once. Just as it had with the doctor. He didn't believe me at first either.

"How come you're so sunburned? Is that make-up?"

I touched my face and said, "It must still be from the summer. It's because of the birds."

"The birds?"

"The ones who come to drink from the leaky faucet on the floor above me. They're used to me by now. Sometimes I sit up there quietly and feed them crumbs. There's a lot of sun up there. Each time I scatter the crumbs closer to me. Some of them already eat from my hand."

I told him about Henryk and the doctor.

"Where is your hideout?"

Now five people knew about it.

He told me to follow him. We climbed up to the loft and he pointed to Number 78 in the distance and asked me if it was the house. I nodded.

"Incredible," he said.

We climbed back down and he told the whole story, in low tones, to his wife. Then they sat me down at the table and gave me food. A real, hot meal: soup and meat and vegetables and pudding and bread. Wow, did I eat! I could hardly get up from the table afterward. Not that I was on the verge of starvation. But I hadn't seen food like that for a long time. I was as hungry as a wolf for it.

They kept whispering to each other while I ate. It worried me a bit. But they didn't look like types who would have me turned in. And soon they let me in on the secret.

"Alex," said Bolek. "You'll stay with us. We'll go get your friend and bring him somewhere safe. And you'll be here with us. We'll arrange papers for you."

"It's no problem," said his wife. "I have a nephew who looks like you and lives in a village not far from here. Bolek will get his birth certificate and documents. You'll be him, staying with us. You'll even go to school. How about it?"

She had a pleasant, chirpy voice.

I wanted so much to say yes. I really liked them. The woman had kind eyes. And Bolek had brains. I had already asked him if he was a teacher before the war. He wasn't. He was a political organizer. A Communist. One of those who wanted everyone to be equal. Even workers. And who didn't hate Jews. That's what he told me.

"I can't stay," I said sadly.

"Why not?" both cried at once.

"I'm waiting for my father," I said.

Bolek wanted to say something, but his wife restrained him with her hand. She didn't say a word herself. She just made me a package of some apples she had gotten from her sister in the country. And she wrapped a jar of honey in a newspaper and told me to be careful not to break it.

"Don't worry, ma'am," I said.

If only she knew how many jars of jam and chicken fat I'd carried by the sackful to my hideout without breaking them — except for one time when I was in such a hurry that I forgot to pad them with rags and they cracked.

Bolek walked up and down in the room until I had finished eating and was ready to go. Then he said to me, "Listen carefully, Alex. Every afternoon when the church bells ring for prayer, my wife or my son or I will go up to the loft and look at your house. If you ever need help, you'll signal us." He paused to think. "What's the highest window you can get to?"

I told him.

"All right. The signal will be a board or a pole placed diagonally in it. No one will suspect anything. It will just look as though something in the building fell down. I'll come for you the same day, if I can. And if I can't, someone else will. Don't forget."

I nodded.

"I want you to know that sooner or later the ghetto will be opened up to Poles. They'll take down the ghetto wall and divide up all the apartments. You won't be able to lift a finger then."

"But I will be able to put a pole in the window," I said.

We lifted up our collars and walked as fast as we could, sticking close to the houses. The sleet had changed again to a cold, driving rain that blew now and then in our faces.

The rain grew heavier, and we stopped for a while in a doorway. There was a crowd of people there. At first I thought they were taking cover from the rain too. But then I realized that there must have been a fight, because people were shouting and arguing.

"What happened, Pani?" Bolek asked a woman.

"We found some kikes hiding with the landlord and turned them in. The bastard jeopardized our lives. Raising our rent all the time wasn't enough for him."

Bolek spit angrily on the ground. The woman must have thought that it was on account of the Jews, but I knew that it was on account of her. I wouldn't have minded spitting myself.

We hurried on past the doctor's house. Of course, there was no chance of meeting Stashya now. But on Monday, if it didn't rain, we had a date. Provided she kept it, of course.

Bolek and the doorman of the house with the passage seemed to know each other well. They exchanged a few words, and then Bolek paid him and sent me to get Henryk.

"We'll have a look at him, and hear what he has to say, and then we'll see. One way or another, we'll have him out of the ghetto tonight. Meanwhile, you can tell him to wait for me in the space between the cellars. Get it?"

I got it. Bolek followed me down to the cellar, moved the chest of drawers, and replaced it behind me. Before I waved good-bye to him from the passage he whispered again, "Don't forget our signal, Alex. And here, take some money."

"I don't need any," I whispered back. "The shopping on our side of the wall still isn't so good."

He laughed. I hadn't wanted to take his money. For the moment I preferred taking Henryk's.

I told Henryk what Bolek had said and explained to him what to do. He got to his feet, shivering from the cold. I climbed to the top floor and brought down the heavy winter coat that I had been saving for father. He put it on gladly. And it really made him look better, not quite so scrawny and miserable. I filled his pockets with sugar cubes. He didn't want to take them. He didn't believe me when I told him that I had more on the top floor, but neither did he have the strength to climb up and check for himself.

"Come on," I said.

"No," he said. "I'll go alone."

I couldn't let him do that. I knew the passageways well, while he had never been through them before. He and his friends had simply run straight up Bird Street when they came to join the uprising. Besides which, I couldn't spare him a flashlight, because one set of batteries had gone dead long ago. To say nothing of the pistol. We argued a while and Henryk gave in.

We didn't talk on the way. Each time we passed from house to house we stopped to listen. Henryk was much more careful than I, even though, looking out in recent days from the stairs of the house next door, I had seen policemen escorting officials with stacks of papers in their hands. They must have been drawing up lists of the houses and apartments that were to be given out to the Poles.

We reached 32 Bakers Street. I moved the chest of drawers and squeezed for a minute with Henryk into the space between the cellars.

"Let me leave you some money," he suddenly said.

I'd almost forgotten to ask for it. He took out his wad of bills and divided it in half.

"That's too much," I said.

"Shut up and take it," he said. "I have more."

He showed me another wad of bills hidden in an inner pocket. I thanked him for the money and we said good-bye. I gave him my hand and he shook it firmly. Then I shook his hand back as hard as I could and we parted like men. That is, he really was one. So was I, except for my voice, which hadn't yet begun to change.

17

Winter

It snowed all night long, the first snow of the year. In the morning, I decided that I simply had to go to the park that afternoon. But on my way down the ladder for my daily visit to the house next door I saw the paw prints of a dog in the white blanket of snow that covered the ruins below. I had never noticed dogs in the building before. Could it have smelled something that I ate last night? I descended as far as the bottom rung and caught myself. If a dog left tracks, so would I — and anyone entering the building would see them leading to and from my hideout. After that it would simply be a matter of putting two and two together. I'd only be free to come and go when a heavy enough snow was falling to cover my tracks right away.

I climbed back up to the bottom floor to think. The note I'd left father was snowed under: I'd have to draw new arrows and hide the "treasure" again by the front gate, which was sheltered from the snow by the entranceway above it. But even so, how could I step in the snow, if only to go next door, without leaving tracks?

I pulled the ladder around to the wall and climbed down

again. If I moved with great care, now I could work my way along the base of the wall where no snow had fallen or would fall unless the wind shifted. And I needn't worry that father might have come in the night and not found my note, because then his footprints would be visible too. I felt proud of myself for having thought of all that and told Snow that I could have been an Indian scout.

In the afternoon, I crossed over to the Polish side, paid the doorman, and headed straight for the park. A lot of the boys I'd played football with were there again. By now I knew most of them. We had a big snowball fight. At first it was a free-for-all, but then we chose sides. A boy named Wlodek suggested that we play Germans and Poles, but no one wanted to be a German, so we decided to be two teams without names. Mine and Wlodek's. Suddenly I had become a captain.

We had a real snow war. I was so wet when it was over that I actually shook with cold. It was beginning to get dark out. Everyone went home. I knew what would happen to me when I got back to the ghetto and I fought to hold it in until then. The gate of the house on the Polish side was closed but not locked. It creaked on its hinges and I slipped inside and went down to the cellar. I think the doorman saw me from his window, but he didn't come out or call to me. It was a good thing that the entrance to the cellar was right by the gate, so that tenants looking down into the courtyard couldn't see me. Perhaps that's why the building had been chosen in the first place.

I worked my way back up Bird Street, gritting my teeth. Not because I was cold but because of the sobs that kept wanting to burst from my throat. Each time I passed from house to house I had to remind myself to stop and listen. At every opening, in every passageway, I told myself, "Take it easy, Alex. Move quietly. Otherwise you'll be discovered." And I kept having to say to myself too, sometimes even talking half out loud, "Don't cry yet. You mustn't cry here. Wait till you're back in the larder, under the pillows. Only there."

I forced myself to keep it in. By the time I got back to Number 78 a thick, quiet snow was falling again. The flakes were big and soft. I cut straight across the ruins to my hide-out. The snow would cover my tracks in no time. I climbed up the ladder, almost forgetting to pull it up after me. That had never happened to me before. I shut myself in the larder, buried my head under the pillows, and burst into tears.

Gradually it passed. I covered the air vent and lit the burner. First I warmed my hands over it; then I took off my wet clothes and hung them up to dry. I boiled water for tea, drank it through a sugar cube, and fed Snow. I didn't talk to him, though. I couldn't tell him what had happened. I was afraid that if I did the crying would start all over again.

I stayed home for the next four days, until Monday. It was a fine winter day, and not so cold. I paid the doorman and smiled at him when he wagged his finger at me. I went straight to the park again. The boys were playing hide-and-seek. Stashya was there too. She was the only girl and hadn't joined the game. I said hello to her. She nodded to me.

"Your girlfriend?" asked Wlodek.

At first I was angry and wanted to tell him to mind his own business, but then I thought again. Mother used to say that whenever I was mad I should count to ten before speaking. For the first time that I could remember I took her advice. And it worked. I smiled at him and shook my head up and down. He gave a knowing laugh. Suddenly we were friends, as though we shared a secret. Maybe he too had expected me to say something nasty and was pleasantly surprised.

I played with them. She stood to one side and watched for a while, and then turned to go. I ran after her and shouted, "Stashya!"

She waited for me to catch up.

The boys began to yell that I was quitting in the middle of the game. But Wlodek made them pipe down and said in a loud voice, "Leave him alone!"

Then he said something else in a low voice that made them laugh. But at least they didn't bother us anymore.

We decided to go see if the little swan pond had frozen over and if anyone was skating on it. We walked very slowly, without saying a word. Suddenly I felt embarrassed. Maybe she did too. Except that I knew that what I felt was not really embarrassment. What it was was not being able to talk to her about anything that I really wanted to. And having to make believe. It was better to say nothing.

It was lovely in the park. The snow had been cleared from all the main paths but was still fresh and white. A mother and some children had built a big snowman together, using coals for the eyes. And then Stashya asked me the one question that I was most afraid of, "Where do you live, Alex?"

"Not far away. On the other side of the park."

"On Poplar Street?"

She wanted to know. Maybe she wanted to meet my parents or come visit me. Or just to wait for me some time in the street. I knew then that we could never meet again.

"Let's start back," I said.

She began to tell me about herself. About her school. About her teacher. About a girl called Marisha who was her best friend in her class. About how she had no friends in her building because the children her age were all boys and the girls were either too young or too old. And about a poor little girl on her block who hung out all day long in the street in all but the worst weather. I almost told her that I knew all about her.

"Look, the reason that I can't tell you where I live is that I'm . . ." I stopped automatically. I simply couldn't get out the word. It was so forbidden. So dangerous. One small word that could cost you your life. She looked at me with her dark blue eyes. She was the prettiest girl I'd ever met. And then I told her.

She turned red all over.

"Do you hate Jews?"

She bowed her head.

"I mean, would you turn me in? You know, you only have to mention it to your parents without thinking and that could be the end of me. I told you the truth just now because I couldn't lie. But now we'll have to say good-bye and not meet anymore. And you'll have to pretend not to know me, even if some day you should see me walk down your street."

I was already sorry I had told her. What a dope I had been. I had ruined everything. I should never have done it. Never, never, never!

I hadn't even said good-bye to her. As though it were her fault. Suddenly she called after me, "Alex!"

I walked back to her.

She was Jewish too! I couldn't believe it. I just kept staring at her. How was it possible? Could she have made it up just to keep me from worrying?

"Is your mother your real mother?"

"Yes."

She began to tell me her true story. Little by little I came to believe her. She too knew that she had broken the most sacred rule and done what must never be done, no matter what. Not until the war was over. I saw how pale she grew as she told me.

"You can trust me," I said.

Then I told her about myself. From the beginning. By now I was an old hand at it. Her eyes sparkled while she listened. She was so glad that I "lived" right across from her. She didn't ask me any questions or say anything. I didn't tell her about the pistol. And then we saw that everyone in the street was hurrying home. It was getting dark. The curfew was about to begin. She was frightened.

"My mother will kill me!" she said. "She'll make me stay home for a whole week. She must be worried to death. I'm not allowed to be out after dark. What have I done?"

"Run right home," I said. "We'll meet again next Monday."

"I'll be looking . . . ," she leaned forward and whispered in my ear, ". . . at the air vent under your window."

"Try to sit at your window, too, as often as you can," I said.

* * *

As soon as I got back I opened the air vent and looked through my binoculars. She had raised the blackout curtain on her window. Inside her room was still dark, but I was sure that she had done it for me.

I gave Snow a big meal that evening. I had a lot to tell him. Sometimes I was glad that he was only a mouse. That way I could tell him anything I wanted.

 **18**

The Nicest Day

All week long I thought of Stashya and watched her when she was at her window. She did what I had asked her to and sat reading there all the time. Now I shook with anger whenever I saw Yanek, the bully, start up with her on her way to school. I'd make him pay for it one day. Although looking at her, I wasn't sure that it really bothered her that much. Sometimes I had the feeling that she actually enjoyed it, and that made me even madder.

I would have given anything for a telephone. One connected just to her. I tried to think of ways we could communicate. I had all kinds of crazy, impossible thoughts that I told to Snow. I'll bet he was laughing at me inside. The more I thought about it, though, the clearer it was to me that there was no way of talking to her without risking being caught. The biggest chance I could take would be to signal her by opening and closing the air vent. Once would mean yes, twice would mean no, and three times would mean I don't know. But how would she see the vent open and close? I knew that it could hardly be made out at all from her house, especially when Number 78 was in shadow.

I would have to give her my binoculars. But no, I wasn't ready to part with them even for her! And then I had an idea. I could give her half of them. I checked and saw that they could be taken apart. Each of us would have one lens. It wouldn't be quite the same as before, because you couldn't see as well with one eye as you could with two, everything seemed flatter, but it was the only way.

Next I thought of how she could send me messages. I tried to invent my own system, but in the end the simplest thing, even though it took lots of dots and dashes to make one word, was Morse code, which I had learned in the Boy Scouts. I would tell her to wave her hands. A right-hand wave would be a dash and a left-hand wave would be a dot.

But then why couldn't I use Morse code too by opening and closing the air vent either quickly or slowly? I could, but it seemed too risky. True, the vent was hard to make out, but that was when it was still. If someone kept moving it back and forth, it was likely to attract attention. Which was a shame, because it meant that we wouldn't be able to have a real conversation. Still, it was better than nothing. And in an emergency I could use Morse, too. Meanwhile Stashya could send me short messages. For instance, when to meet her. Or that she couldn't keep a date. Or that she loved me. Would she really ever want to tell me that? I hoped so. I got all tingly just thinking about it, although I wasn't sure I'd have the courage to tell her.

At last it was Monday again. I had been worried all week, because every day I had seen officials making their rounds with their lists. And as long as they were in the ghetto Stashya couldn't signal me at all, because her strange movements might be noticed. And what if the ghetto should suddenly be opened to Poles? What if they took down the wall? It seemed impossible, against the laws of nature. If it happened I might be able to cross over to the Polish side without having to pay the doorman. Yet on the other hand, I might not be able to go anywhere at all.

The doorman had raised his price. The louse! But I didn't argue with him. I had to stay on his good side. He told me that one of the tenants had gotten suspicious and had to be paid off now. Maybe that was even the truth. There were rats everywhere.

I arrived in the park at the same time of the afternoon as I had the week before. In the distance I heard music from the skating pond. My gang of friends wasn't there. The skate concession was open and the brass trumpet of the gramophone was already screwed into its hole in the wall. Once I had thought that it was made of gold. Skaters glided over the ice. Before we moved to the ghetto I used to come and rent skates from the concession owners. They made a hole in the bottom of your heels, if you didn't already have one, and attached the skates with metal taps and shoemaker's nails. Besides the entrance fee, you were charged for the work and an hourly rate for the skates.

I loved the music. When I was little, I would come not just to skate but also to watch the fat woman crank the handle of the gramophone. I was fascinated by the quickly spinning record and by the iron needle that stuck out from its shiny head and coaxed melodies from the round, black disk as if by magic.

For a second, I was afraid I would be recognized. But there was no chance of that. I was bigger now and dressed differently. No chance at all.

The fat woman I remembered wasn't there. Instead there were two older men and a young hunchback who helped them. I asked if they rented skates.

"Do you have money?" they asked suspiciously.

"Yes."

"Let's see your heels."

I showed them my heels.

"We'll have to make holes in them. Does your mother allow it?"

"Of course," I said. "She wouldn't have given me the money if she didn't."

The hunchback sat me down on a high chair and went to get his tools.

"Just a minute," I said. "I'm going to get my sister."

I returned to the middle of the park. Stashya was waiting with her back to me. I snuck up behind her and said boo. She was frightened. Then she burst out laughing and blushed. She was the most beautiful girl I had seen in my life.

"Let's go skating," I said.

"But I don't know how."

"I'll teach you," I said. "And there are chairs for beginners."

Beginners held on to little chairs and pushed them ahead of them on the ice until they felt ready to let go. That's when the fun began — especially when some lady in a dress would fall down with her legs in the air. Even the grown-ups laughed then.

"But I don't have any skates. What's wrong with you, Alex?"

I explained that they could be rented. And that her heels would have holes made in them.

"My mother will have a fit when she sees them," she said. I could see that she was weakening.

"She won't. Just keep the bottoms of your heels on the floor. She doesn't shine your shoes for you, does she?"

"No, I do."

She agreed. I told her that from now on she was my sister.

"But all the kids know already."

I shrugged. What difference did it make?

We sat down and the hunchback drilled holes in our heels. It tickled our feet. Then he held each foot on his knee as though he were shoeing a horse and drove in the nails. I was afraid he might drive them into my foot, but he laughed and showed me how short they were. He held them in his mouth and took them out one by one like an upholsterer. I always got a kick out of that. It was like watching a sword swallower in the circus.

I paid for everything in advance. I had prepared the money in a separate pocket, so that I didn't have to flash the whole wad that Henryk had given me. It was too bad that I hadn't stashed it in my hideout with the pistol, which I left behind because last time it kept getting in my way. All during the football game I had to check that it wasn't falling out of my pocket and that none of the boys could see it.

That day was the nicest of my life. At least since I had been living alone. The nicest afternoon, anyway. I tightened Stashya's laces, helped her on with her skates, and tightened them too with a key. Then she held on to my arm and I gave her a chair, led her on to the ice, and skated slowly by her side. After a while Wlodek showed up with two of his friends and challenged me to a competition. I hadn't skated in over a year, but I still was pretty good, even on one leg. They watched me admiringly.

"Where were you all week?"

"My mother's been sick."

"Come visit me sometime," said Wlodek. "I've got lots of toys. Even some new ones that my father got off the Jews."

"All right."

"And I'll come visit you, too."

"All right."

What would he say if he were to see my "house"? I bet he'd want to run away. Maybe not, though, because he seemed to have guts. But it was obvious that things couldn't go on like this much longer. Sooner or later something would keep me from crossing over. The Poles would move into the ghetto or God knows what. Though I didn't think it would happen as fast as it actually did.

Wlodek and his friends didn't tease me over Stashya. At first they smiled at each other, but when I smiled too, they left us alone. Just once I heard one of them say, "They're like a real married couple."

Maybe we'd be one after the war. Who knew?

Stashya learned fast. After a while she let go of her chair and gave me her hand. And fell down. I couldn't help laughing. Neither could she. Then she fell again, this time nearly pulling me with her. So I gave her both my hands and skated backward, holding on to her. That was better. Until she fell again and I went down with her.

We skated for two whole hours. Two hours that were my treat. Until she said she had to go home. After last Monday her mother had really kept her in the whole week. She had been both worried and angry.

I couldn't blame her.

I walked Stashya home. We laughed all the way at every little thing. Until I noticed that Yanek was behind us.

"Yanek's following us," I whispered.

She stopped laughing. "I'd better get home fast before he starts up," she said.

We said good-bye. She continued straight ahead and I turned around and started back, passing Yanek without looking at him. I didn't hurry. I just looked over my shoulder after a while and saw that he still was behind me. I was glad that I'd given Stashya her half of the binoculars before leaving the park. I stopped. He drew closer and stopped too.

"So you're new around here, hey?"

"It's none of your business."

"Suppose it is?"

"You don't own this street."

"We'll see about that," he said with a nasty smile.

I shrugged and kept walking. What would I do if he didn't leave me? I decided to head back to the park. It was getting late and Wlodek and his friends would be gone by now.

"What do you want from me?"

"I want to see where you live, Jew-boy."

"You're a Jew-boy yourself. Come on, I'll show you where I live. And my brother the policeman will show you something else that you won't forget either."

I knew exactly what I was going to do. I would turn in at the first gate without a doorman and then, if he was still following me, I'd sock him as hard as I could in the face and again in the stomach, in the place that father called the solar plexus. It was the only way to get rid of him. Maybe it wasn't nice to do a sneaky thing like that instead of challenging him to a fair fight, but it was the same as being a gentleman with the Germans. And it would teach him to keep away from Stashya.

Actually, father had taught me to do it the other way around. First let him have it in the stomach; then, when he doubled over, in the face.

He doubled up and fell. I cleared out fast, though not before I saw the blood spurt from his nose. It was already clear to me that this was my last visit on the Polish side. Unless Yanek miraculously disappeared. And even then I wouldn't dare show my face because he'd have told the others about the "new boy," and the next time someone else would be waiting for me. The grocer, for instance. I hadn't liked him from the start. My knuckles were sore for a whole week afterward.

At first I walked slowly. Then I heard shouts and I crossed to the other side of the street and broke into a run. Not a real run. It was more of a skip, the way you run just to show you're feeling good.

It was too bad, though. I still had enough money for two more crossings over at the new price, plus renting skates and two or three more trips to the grocery. And after that I could have tried selling some of the things I had found. I was sure the doorman of the house by the wall would have bought them. I could have started with the suits I'd been saving.

19

The Poles Arrive

Although I always left the faucet slightly open, the water froze in the pipes. They were partly exposed to the air and it had simply gotten too cold. I melted snow on the burner, but I was worried about my kerosene running out. I should have taken more of it. There had certainly been plenty. And what I had might not last me through the winter.

I talked with Stashya. That is, she did the talking. I simply answered yes or no.

She signaled in Morse code: "I love you." It was easier to say that from a distance. For me too. Then she signaled: "Do you love me?" And I signaled back: "Yes." Every morning she waved to me before leaving for school. And every afternoon she sat down to do her homework at the window.

It was exhausting to talk that way. And we were more and more afraid of being seen, because more and more officials were poking around the ghetto.

The Sunday after the run-in with Yanek she tried making a date with me. I answered "I don't know" to every question. It was only the next day that word got out on her

street that the "new boy" was a kike and that, when Yanek
had tried catching him, two other kikes had attacked him,
beaten him up, and run away.

It took her a long while to transmit all that in code, and it
took me a long while to decode it.

"Did you beat him up by yourself?"

"Yes," I signaled back.

"Very good. It's just an awful shame we can't meet. I'm
crying. Are you?"

"No," I signaled. Then: "Yes."

"Has your father come yet?"

A few days before Christmas, our "conversations"
ended. The houses were handed over to the Poles. Early
one morning as I was on my daily visit to the house next
door, I heard people in the street. I peeked out a window
and saw policemen, but they didn't look like a search party.
There were civilians with briefcases, too. Now and then
they checked their papers. And then I heard hammering
from the Polish side and bricks falling and smashing. And a
whoop of voices from the street. The last thing I saw before
returning to my hideout was that the policemen had taken
up positions by the gates of the houses. One policeman to
each gate. And sometimes a civilian, too.

I looked out the air vent. Workers were knocking down
the wall. And people, some of whom I knew by sight, were
jumping for joy. Suddenly they would have a big, wide
street again, just like in the days before the ghetto, and new
neighbors across it instead of empty houses and a wall
topped with glass. Maybe some of them would be moving
into the ghetto themselves. Or maybe they had friends or
relatives who would be. There was a housing shortage because of the war.

I didn't move from my hideout. All week I heard wagons and trucks driving up and down the street. More and more people kept arriving. Moving men yelled and children cried. There were constant quarrels. I saw Stashya. She was standing helplessly in her window. She couldn't signal me anymore, because the new tenants on Bird Street would have noticed it immediately. She could only smile at me once or twice and blow me a kiss to cheer me up.

I was really pretty depressed. The one thing I had had to look forward to in my life was the "conversations" between us. Even if they only amounted to a few words, they were my one contact with the outside world. And now they were over. The wall was gone. And I was surrounded.

I had another problem, too. I couldn't go to the house next door in the morning anymore. The passage had even been sealed. Some tenants must have moved in. As long as it was winter and cold, I didn't worry about it too much. Things just froze anyway. But what would I do when it began to warm up?

And still another thing. I was afraid to climb up to the top floor now for provisions. I would pick the darkest, snowiest nights and go up only after midnight. Each time I took down with me as much stuff as I could. And then one night I saw that there was hardly anything left.

While I was up there, I cleared off the snow onto the ruins below. I knew that snow was heavy because sometimes, if a lot of it fell, it broke the branches of the trees. So that on top of all my other worries, I was now afraid that the floor above me would collapse and bring my floor crashing down too. I had taken to keeping the free end of my emergency rope in the larder with me. If worse came to worse I could try to escape out the window. It wouldn't be easy with freezing hands, but I could do it if I had to. What a dope I had been not to have looked for a pair of gloves!

Before long the new children on the street began to play in the ruins. Just like we had. The grown-ups would run after them and drag them out with screams and shouts. At night I heard steps and whispers. The building must have become a meeting place for crooks or smugglers. Sometimes big kids who had stolen or bought cigarettes without permission, or even rolled their own from butts collected in the street, would come to smoke in the darkness before the curfew began. On cloudy nights it was so pitch-dark because of the blackout that I could lie at the edge of the floor without moving and listen to them talk. When I was no longer afraid to listen in on the children like that, I began to eavesdrop on the grown-ups too, lying on my stomach bundled up against the cold. Some of them were really smugglers who had plans to break through to the cellar, which they remembered from the days before the war, in order to store their goods there. And once some members of the underground came looking for a place to hide. Before I could make up my mind to throw them down the ladder, they were gone. Bolek had told me that not every member of the Polish underground could be trusted. The Communists were generally all right, but the right-wingers hated Jews as much as the Germans. If a Jew tried joining the partisans in the forests and fell into their hands, they would kill him without thinking twice. I guess they were skunks like Yanek, just bigger.

The one thing I didn't have to worry about now was making tracks in the snow. The ruins were full of them. But

I didn't dare leave my hideout, though my feet were itching to get out.

Christmas came and went and New Year's Eve arrived. All night I heard music coming from the bar on Stashya's street. She had told me that it was a nightclub for German officers, who were the only people allowed out during curfews. The Germans kept coming and going. Each time the door opened and light fell on the street, I could see the officers inside and their fancy ladies sitting with them in fur collars. At midnight they opened the door and turned out all the lights, and when the crazy woman's grandfather clock began to toll twelve with all the church bells, they burst into a loud cheer. Then they turned the lights back on and shut the door again. Too bad they did. A new year had begun: 1944. Perhaps the year in which the war would end. The year that everyone hoped for. Even the Germans. Except that they hoped the war would end differently.

Soon afterward I heard someone stomping loudly about in the ruins, as if he were trying to be heard. I crawled out of the larder. The man switched on a flashlight and shone it around the building, like someone looking for something. Then he shone it on himself. It was Bolek.

"Alex?" he whispered.

"I'm here," I whispered back.

"I've come to get you."

"I'm sorry," I said, feeling a catch in my heart. "I can't go."

"You can't go on staying here, you pighead."

I didn't answer.

"I've brought you a package. Throw me down a rope. If

anyone enters the building, throw me the other end too. I'll be all right. And don't forget the pole in the window!"

I threw down a rope and hauled up the package that he tied to it. It was full of goodies. I gave a little of everything to Snow and we celebrated the new year together. Bolek had taken a big risk by breaking the curfew. Perhaps he had purposely picked New Year's Eve, when even policemen and Germans got drunk and weren't so strict about things.

I had another visitor. One day I heard children down below and suddenly I made out Stashya's voice. She was talking louder than usual. I guessed it was so I would hear. But she had more in mind than just that.

When it got dark and the children went home, I crawled out of my larder to have a look. She was still there, looking back and forth from the gate to my floor. Then she saw me.

"We're moving to the country," she whispered. "Good-bye, Alex."

"When?"

"Tomorrow morning."

"Come on up."

"Someone will see us . . ."

I threw her the ladder. Whatever would be, would be. She climbed up awfully slowly. I had forgotten that I climbed it like that too in the beginning. We were lucky, because as soon as the ladder was back up and we were to-gether in the larder we heard boys' voices below. They must have come for a smoke. I closed the door gently be-hind us. My hinges were well oiled, too.

I didn't light a candle. I lit the flashlight instead and cupped my hand over it to show her where she was. Then she looked out the air vent to see my view of her. She had brought me a letter. At first she had planned to leave it for me down below. It had no date or name on it. And she had brought her half of the binoculars, too.

"No," I whispered. "Keep it to remember me by."

She was worried, because her mother didn't know that she'd gone out.

"They'll leave before the curfew," I whispered.

I wanted to show her Snow. That really shocked her. I almost burst out laughing. I had forgotten that some girls were afraid of mice.

"But he's white," I whispered.

"No, don't," she begged.

"Who are you scared of more, mice or Germans?"

I could feel her smile.

So I showed him to her. She took a peek at him and saw that nothing terrible happened.

"His eyes are like tiny buttons," she said all of a sudden.

"Do you think he's nice?" I asked in a whisper.

"Nice? I guess he is. If only his tail weren't so long . . ."

I closed Snow's box.

"Where are you moving to?"

"Mother has a friend in the country. We're going to stay with her."

"Where in the country?"

She didn't know. Her mother had thought it safer not to tell her.

"How will I find you after the war?"

We tried to think of some way to find each other. Our first thought was to write each other care of the king of England. England was still sure to have a king, even if Buckingham Palace was bombed to bits. Maybe it already had been. But that seemed kind of silly. You couldn't expect a king to concern himself with such things. So then we thought of the Red Cross, in Switzerland. And if the Germans conquered Switzerland, then in Australia. That far they would never get. They were already losing the war.

We settled on the Red Cross. Though just to be sure we decided to meet here too, at 78 Bird Street, on the first New Year's Day after the war.

The boys left the building. We crept cautiously out of the larder. I kissed her and told her that I loved her. She cried.

I let down the ladder for her and told her to count to thirteen, because that's how many rungs it had. And because it was my lucky number. She almost fell in the dark, but in the end she got down safely.

In the morning I watched the wagon come to take her and her mother with all their things. She knew that I was looking. When they started out, she waved to me. And then her mother waved too. That really bowled me over. Could they have been waving to someone else? No, they were looking straight at me. I guessed that after coming home late last night she'd had no choice but to tell her mother the truth.

I didn't open the air vent all that day. I didn't want to have to see who had moved into their apartment. When I looked the next day, though, it was still empty.

It was awfully strange to look at that street that had once been the border between two different worlds. Nothing was left of the wall now. Trolleys ran again on the tracks that had been under it. It was as though the ghetto had never existed. As though other people had never lived in it.

20

Crying Can Be Catching, Just Like Laughter

About two weeks after Stashya and her mother moved out, there was a real blizzard. At first the snow fell steadily all day. From time to time I climbed up to the top floor and cleared it off. Then strong winds began to blow. I thought I would freeze to death in my larder. I took pillows and a big quilt and lined the walls with them. I kept the burner going all the time. And I had a new idea: heating bricks over it. As soon as one brick was hot I took it off and put on another. It was a little like having a brick stove.

I was sure of it now: The kerosene wouldn't last the winter. Meanwhile, though, I didn't want to freeze. I stayed in the larder all that night and the next day, though I was worried about the top floor. It was just too cold to go out. On the third night, the snow kept falling, and in the morning, I suddenly heard a loud rumble and everything swayed back and forth. Something crashed on the ruins below and bricks began to rain down. There were a few more loud thuds, and then it grew quiet again.

The larder that I was in had come through unscathed — at least there was that to be thankful for. I tried opening it.

One of the doors was jammed from the outside. I managed to open the door nearest the rope ladder and breathed a sigh of relief. Most of the floor was still there, though covered with bricks and fallen beams. The top floor had partially collapsed, breaking off a section of my floor as it fell. The rope ladder was buried beneath snow and debris.

I glanced above me to see if the cave-in was over. It was impossible to tell. To be on the safe side, I took a pillow and tied it over my head; if nothing else, it would help keep me warm. Then, without stopping to think, I began to clear all the rubble that I could onto the ruins below. Now and then I paused to look at the gate, although it was hard to believe that anyone would show up in this weather.

And then disaster struck again. Mother always used to say that it came in pairs. I had left the larder door open and a gust of wind blew something against the burner, knocking it over and setting the quilt on fire. I didn't panic. I took a blanket and smothered the flames right away. Father had once told me never to try putting out an oil fire with water, and I guessed that went for snow too. Maybe it didn't, but this was no time to experiment.

Once I had dug out the rope ladder and cleared off the floor, I shut myself back up in the larder. From now on, I thought, I had better be careful and stay away from the edge of the floor.

As soon as the weather improved a bit, the children came back to play. It simply wasn't as cold in the ruins as it was outside in the street. I could tell right away from their voices, though, that something was up. That there had been a change. I opened the larder a crack to try to hear what they were saying. It didn't take long to make out what had happened. The floors that fell had smashed through the ceiling of the cellar and opened up a new hole in it.

The children didn't have much time to enjoy themselves, though. Word quickly got out and some policemen arrived, looked about, and talked and shouted a bit. The next day workers came and bricked up the entrance to the building. Perhaps they used bricks that had come from the wall of the ghetto.

I didn't know whether or not to be sorry. True, Bolek couldn't come to visit me now, but if I signaled him he could always bring a ladder or find some other way of getting in through the second-floor window.

I figured that the crooks might try that too, and so for several days I took care to stay in my hideout. But from the moment the gate was bricked up, the building wasn't entered anymore. Gradually I felt a great relief. Once again I was free to climb down. The ceiling of the cellar where the two floors crashed down on it must have been very thin, because the hole was a big one and the rubble that poured through it made a kind of ramp leading down. It wasn't the easiest descent, but it was manageable. At least I had somewhere to go now and a bathroom to use. Being cooped up in the larder all the time had been awfully depressing.

One morning I was on my way down to the cellar and had already raised the ladder behind me when I heard voices approaching. It sounded as though someone was trying to climb into the building through a window facing Stashya's street. I darted down into the cellar and listened. Someone vaulted inside. Then someone else. They must have gotten in with a ladder. My first impulse was to go a level deeper and hide in the bunker, but I quickly changed my mind. Whoever it was would want to have a look down there. It was better to hide in one of the last storage rooms. They might get to it, too, but I hoped that after seeing several empty rooms before it they would leave it alone.

I heard bricks fall as the two men entered the cellar and slid down the ramp of debris. Had they heard me come down here? I couldn't tell. I could hear their voices now. I guessed that they were standing by the entrance to the bunker.

"Care for a cigarette?"

There was no answer. Just the scratch of a match against a box.

"Want to have a look inside?"

"Yes."

"There's not a thing left here."

I shivered. One of the voices was awfully like father's.

I heard them climb down the wooden stairs into the bunker and make some dull, scraping sounds. Maybe they were moving the benches, or maybe they had found the food cache. Not that there could be any food in it. The Germans had emptied the bunker down to its last crumb before blowing up the entrance.

I have to hear that voice again, I thought. It couldn't be father's. But the man was looking for someone. Maybe it was for someone who had been in the bunker. The voice was so like his. Yet I could be imagining it. Or maybe it was someone else who sounded like him. Anything was possible. I waited tensely. They climbed back up to the cellar, looked in a few storage rooms as I thought they would, and continued back up to the ground floor.

"Shall we go?"

"Let's sit down for a minute."

"Someone will steal the ladder. I'd better pull it inside."

I heard footsteps receding and returning.

"You see, they must have killed him here. I never really thought I'd find him. I just wanted to see the building. Like visiting a cemetery."

"Well, we're not in any hurry," said the second man. "And we had to make this trip into town anyway."

The first man said nothing.

"When is our rendezvous?"

"When it gets dark," said father's voice.

There was silence, except for the usual sounds from the street.

"What did she see?"

"Who?"

"That woman who said she was with them."

"The boy started to run," said father's voice. "A policeman chased him, and the old man tripped him and knifed him."

"And the boy?"

"The boy ran in here. They came in after him and shot him."

I couldn't move. It was all so clear now. Father thought that I was dead. I wanted to run out of the cellar and throw myself on him. Why didn't I, then? Why didn't I at least shout something? It was very simple: Because I no longer believed that he would come. I knew that now. I had stopped believing it long ago. It was just so impossible. I simply hadn't admitted it to myself. I hadn't allowed myself a moment's doubt. It was that belief that kept me going. Only now that it had actually happened, I couldn't believe it. Now that father was sitting so close to me at last, I could finally allow myself to disbelieve.

I forced myself to get up. I forced myself to climb toward them. I made no attempt to move quietly. The two men jumped to their feet. They weren't frightened. They were simply surprised to see me come up from the cellar.

"It's a boy," said the first man.

He was big and broad-shouldered, like father. The two of them were dressed like Polish peasants with short fur coats, fur hats, and boots. Father couldn't recognize me — at least not until I took my hat off, which I was too choked up to do. I knew myself well enough by now to know that I had to cry. And I knew that if I did anything but walk straight toward him I'd burst into tears before I could reach him.

"Alex."

He didn't shout it. He said it in a very strange voice. Maybe that's how a person talks to a ghost.

"Father."

That's really the end of my story. They took me to the forest to be with them, among the partisans. But I can't resist telling you how I pulled down the rope ladder before their astonished eyes, and how I explained to them about the two lines for standing and kneeling that I had drawn on the floor and that couldn't be seen anymore, and how I showed them my hideout, and how I told them everything, right from the beginning: about coming to Number 78, and about first living in the cellar without knowing that there was a bunker beneath me, and about the Gryns not wanting to give me any food, and about the family that took the food I found. I mean that Snow found. I told them about the Polish boys in the park and about the skating pond. And about Stashya.